Moon Music

Moon Music

Aurora Dawning

Moon Music
Copyright © 2016 by Aurora Dawning
All rights reserved.

No part of this publication may be reproduced, distributed, or transmitted in any form or by any means, including photocopying, recording, or other electronic or mechanical methods, without the prior written permission of the publisher, except in the case of brief quotations embodied in critical reviews and certain other noncommercial uses permitted by copyright law. For permission requests, write to the publisher, addressed "Attention: Permissions Coordinator," at the publishers address below.

This is a work of fiction. Names, characters, events are the products of the author's imagination or used in a fictitious manner. Any resemblance to actual persons, living or dead, or actual events is purely coincidental.

ISBN-13: 978-0-9906640-6-2
ISBN-10: 0-9906640-6-6
Library of Congress Control Number: 2016941553

Cover Copyright © 2016 Aurora Dawning
Cover Art by Cline Covers & Design
Book design and production by Gray Dog Press, Spokane, WA

Published by
Bratcher Publishing
30007 N Miller Lane
Chattaroy, WA 99003

Acknowledgments

THEY SAY NO MAN is an island. That's especially true for writers. I am so grateful for all the support, encouragement, and friendship from so many wonderful people:

Virginia, Jamie, Tina, Terri, Gayle, Pat, Linda, Frostine, Sharon, Will, Caroline, Annette, Betty, Bill, Cherise, Sue, Mitzi, Marnie, Kate, Tawana, Steve, Stan, Kendra, Sandy, Carmen, Larry, Lorena, Nancy, Warwick, Barb, Ron, Randy, and Ruth.

Everyone at Bratcher Publishing, the Tin Pencil Writers Group and Liberty Lake Writers Group,

Michelle, my wonderful graphic artist,

All the musicians who have inspired and influenced me,

And especially to my family, both the living and those who have passed from this life.

With special thanks to all those involved in animal rescue and adoption efforts, everywhere.

Prologue

Gina Marie Thompson always knew she had been born under a full moon.

On her seventh birthday, her grandmother whispered, "Gina, you're not old enough to understand yet, but being born under a full moon can be a blessing. It's the end of one cycle, but the beginning of another. The moon is the most beautiful and powerful at that time. There's magic in it."

As usual, there seemed to be a secret message encrypted in the words. Gina adored everything about her grandmother, including the mysterious way she had of sometimes knowing about things before they happened. The happiest days of her childhood were spent in her grandmother's simple little house where love wrapped around her in layers of warmth. That warmth quickly evaporated when she entered her family's much larger, lavish home.

Gina arrived as a late-in-life baby, unexpected and unwelcome, a subject of seemingly complete indifference by her slim, stylish mother. Margaret Elizabeth Thompson was active in society and served on several important committees. Fredrick Thompson was vice-president of a mining corporation, one of the largest in the world. He traveled extensively, often away for weeks at a time. Her two older brothers were already in college when she was born.

Shy and awkward, Gina cringed in the presence of her mother, who was quick to point out every fault or mistake she made, correcting her speech or dress as she deemed necessary. Gina was in awe and fear of her.

She was frequently hidden from view when her parents entertained, kept behind closed doors washing dishes and glasses as tables were cleared. Sometimes her mother swooped into the closed-off kitchen to supervise, resplendent in one of her formal gowns and glittering diamonds. These sudden appearances made Gina so nervous that once when she was twelve, she dropped a glass on the floor, where it shattered. Margaret marched across the floor and slapped her, hard. "How can you be so clumsy? Those glasses are Waterford Crystal!"

Gina reeled from both her mother's anger and from the sting of the slap on her cheek. Her eyes began to tear. "I'm sorry. I didn't mean to…" she began.

"Just watch what you're doing and don't be so clumsy!" Margaret hissed. She whirled abruptly and flounced to the door, opening it enough to peek out into the living room where guests waited. She turned back to Gina. "Clean this mess up! And turn off the tears!" She paused a moment to position a smile onto her face before she walked through the door, pulling it tightly closed behind her.

Gina dropped to the floor to gather up the pieces of broken glass, cutting her fingers. She watched blood ooze from the cuts and could no longer hold back her tears. She allowed herself to cry, but made sure that no one could hear.

She held up a large piece of broken glass. Facets in the crystal caught the light, flashing a display of colors against the wall. Pretty but cold. *Like mother.* Outside the kitchen window, a pale golden moon floated in the sky, beautiful and warmer than any of the colors in her mother's house.

As Gina grew up, she immersed herself in books, where she always felt welcome and connected to the people in the stories. It was a good way to escape the isolation. She often thought of herself as a kind of ghost, drifting through the house, not a part of the family, not connected, not seen, not noticed, not heard, not appreciated, and unworthy of being loved.

She turned to her grandmother for comfort. "I've never been sure what my mother wanted me to be. All I know is that I'm not it." She brushed tears from her eyes. "Will my life always be like this? You told me I was born under a full moon. Does that mean I will be unlucky all my life?"

"No, Gina. That part is up to you. If you were on a journey to go somewhere, and you were never given a road map, don't you think you would have to figure out how to get there on your own? It seems to me that you must decide who you want to be and what will make you happy."

"I don't understand."

Her grandmother finished a row of knitting before she continued. "Think about the moon, Gina. Sometimes the moon is clouded or hidden, and sometimes it shines so brightly it dazzles. But it is always there. Life is like that, too, sometimes in shadow and sometimes radiant. You have an equal chance for it to be magic, or tragic. Ultimately it's your choice, Gina. Life is what you make it. Will you choose a path that will fulfill you, and make you shine, or will you make unwise choices that will diminish your chance for happiness?"

* * *

Years later, when Gina went away to college, she and her mother were nearly strangers, seeing each other only at Christmas or school breaks.

In college, she discovered a talent for marketing and advertising, and graduated with a degree in business. She applied for and received an internship with the upscale department store chain La Mode Paris, and quickly established herself as a top sales person with a flair for merchandising. At the end of her internship, she was offered a position as an assistant manager. Six months later, she was promoted to department manager.

Her joy was shattered with the news that her grandmother had suffered a stroke, leaving her bedridden. Gina rushed to the hospital, knowing there wasn't much time.

"Only a few minutes," the doctor cautioned. "She's very weak."

Gina opened the door to a small room painted in cheerful shades of blue. A solitary, shrunken figure lay in a hospital bed. The room was quiet except for the hushed whooshing sounds of an oxygen machine. Through the window outside, a fading moon stubbornly resisted the advances of the rising sun. *It's just like she said. Either in brilliance or shadow, the moon is always there.*

Gina crossed the room and reached for her grandmother's hands. The beloved, familiar blue eyes opened. "Gina," she breathed.

"Grandmother, I came as soon as I heard. How are you feeling?"

"Gina, I'm dying."

"No, please don't go," Gina choked in a sob.

Her grandmother struggled to speak. She swallowed several times and rasped out, "Gina, I don't want to leave you, but it's my time." She drew a ragged breath. "Don't be sad. I have lived long enough to see you grow into the beautiful woman you are. Never let anyone make you feel like anything less."

"But what will I do without you? You're the only one I could always count on; the one who loved me." Tears rained down Gina's face. "I'll miss you so much."

In the quiet room, the only sounds were the click and whoosh of the oxygen machine and the bleep of a monitor.

The old lady whispered, "Sweetie, you won't be alone. You have your life, your friends, and a good career." She smiled and her eyes twinkled. She attempted to sit up but could not.

With great difficulty, she continued. "And someday, someone will find you. Someone who can see the beauty inside you. Someone who will help you shine. You will help him shine, too."

"How will I know?"

"Don't worry. You'll know. I think he will come into your life when you least expect it. Good things sometimes come in the most unusual packages. Don't be afraid to take chances." Her voice was barely audible.

She peered up and her hand fluttered down over Gina's. "Always remember who you are, Gina. I am proud of you and I love you." Her eyes crinkled in a loving smile. She sighed and closed her eyes, and she was gone.

Chapter 1

Summer—Phoenix

"WHACK IT ALL OFF, TINA," Gina insisted.

"Are you sure you know what you're doing?" Lynn's voice drawled from the next chair. "Once it's cut, you can't just glue it back on again."

Gina turned to look at her friend. "I know. Go ahead, Tina. I want a completely new look. Something like this." She pointed to a photo in a magazine.

Tina studied the picture for a few minutes. "This is kind of a stacked bob, with a lot of layers. Very modern. It's a good look for blonde hair like yours."

Gina nodded. "I think so, too. I'm going to a party tonight and I'm tired of dealing with all this long hair. It's time for a change."

"Sounds like there might be a man involved," Tina commented as she separated Gina's hair into sections.

"What makes you say that?"

"Oh, I see it all the time. If a woman wears her hair the way her man likes it, and they break up, she gets it cut. Kind of like getting her own identity back."

Lynn laughed. "That's interesting. I never thought about it before, but I think you're right."

"You sound like you might be from someplace down South," Tina suggested.

"Yeah. I'm a Texas girl, born and raised on a ranch."

"Lynn's been my best friend for a long time," Gina said. "I can always count on her to be there for me. That's more than I can say for Terry, who's supposed to be my special somebody."

At the mention of Terry's name, she saw Lynn roll her eyes and make a face. "Terry!" she snorted.

Aurora Dawning

"Lynn doesn't like him," Gina explained. "Maybe she's right. It's exhausting to be around him. Like tap dancing across a mine field. I'm tired of him constantly telling me how I should look, and what he likes. The hell with what he likes! Maybe he should think about what I like for once, and get rid of his spare tire and shave off that ridiculous fringe he likes to wear around his chin."

"Amen to that!" Tina agreed. "I don't know what's gotten into so many men today, why they think that look is attractive. It's ridiculous. Almost like they're all saying 'Look at me! I'm a man! I can grow facial hair!'"

"Thank God they all don't look like that," Lynn snapped. She rolled her eyes again. "I want to see a man's face, not some bushy fringe. Why, if Mike ever tried that, the next meal he'd get from me would be a razor on a plate. He'd know pretty quick that I mean business."

At this, they all laughed. Lynn went back to reading her magazine, and the only sound in the salon was the snipping of hair.

"Well, are you ready for the big reveal?" Tina asked when she was finished. She handed Gina a large mirror.

"Sure," Gina gulped. "Let's see the new me." She sucked in her breath quickly and took a peek.

"I love it!" she exclaimed immediately. "Just love it! It's so short and cutting-edge looking." She pulled up a few strands to give it a spiked look. "Really cool! I can finally wear earrings that won't be hidden under hair." She turned her head from side to side, admiring the cut. "Tina, you're a hairdressing goddess! Thank you!"

"This style will show up those huge eyes of yours a lot more," Lynn suggested.

"Yeah. And I want some dangle earrings. Maybe I'll make some. I've been thinking about designing a cascade of little silver stars falling from a crescent moon." She sketched out her idea and showed it to Lynn.

"Very nice," Lynn approved. "You should do it. I think all the stars would really catch the light."

"So do I," Gina agreed. "I have a few other ideas like this, too. I'm thinking about calling it my 'Starstruck' Collection.

"Pretty cool," Tina commented. "I like the stars, too. I think they would sell."

* * *

At the party, Gina did her best to mingle with the various wives and girlfriends, but always, when she glanced up, Terry was watching. She smiled and tried to be charming, but the stress of worrying about Terry's approval was exhausting. She was careful to eat as little as possible, and had one drink only, sipping it slowly through the afternoon. It would not do for her to seem anything less than at the top of her game.

She wandered over to the barbecue pit, where a group of men stood talking. Terry had his back to her, and was engaged in a lively discussion about something that appeared to be funny. She overheard comments about cars, mixed with crude jokes and something about "chasing skirt."

Gina started to walk away, but just then Terry noticed her. He hurried over and grabbed her wrist.

"What are you doing, Gina?" He leaned closer and tightened his grip.

"Nothing. Someone asked me to check on how much more time before we can eat." It was a lie, but it sounded reasonable. Terry glared at her for a few seconds, then relaxed and let her go.

He smiled over at the women and called out "Shouldn't be too much longer, ladies."

Fake smile. Like a politician. And maybe I'm an idiot to be here with him.

Later, one of the wives noticed Gina's earrings.

"Oh, these are one of my own designs," Gina admitted shyly. "I've been making jewelry for a while, and I'm planning to start my own business. There are a couple of boutiques over in Scottsdale that said they're interested, so it's a start."

The women crowded around to get a better look. Gina blushed at being the recipient of so many friendly comments. Then she noticed Terry.

He looks furious. I wonder what that's about. What did I do to set him off this time?

On the way home, Terry scowled as he drove, saying nothing.

I guess I might as well find out what's on his mind, and get it over with. "That was a really nice party, Terry," she ventured.

Terry glared at her with venom in his expression. "How could you embarrass me like that?" he exploded.

"What are you talking about?"

He snorted. "I take you out to meet my friends. I expect you to look pretty and make me look good. You need to keep your mouth shut. And, you went and got all your hair cut off. I don't like it. I want my woman to look like a woman, not a tomboy."

"Well, I like it. It's edgy and modern. I think it shows off my eyes a lot more this way."

"I don't like it," he snarled. "Then you show me up with your ideas about starting your own business. Designing jewelry! You don't know what you're talking about. I'm an advertising executive, so I know what it takes. If you really want to do jewelry in a big way, you'll have to have production done in the Orient. Otherwise, you'll be stuck selling only to small stores. You should stick to what you know."

"And what is that exactly?"

"Take my advice. Act like I expect you to. Look the way I like."

"So, you want me to be an ornament? What about creativity? What about making something beautiful? Artistic expression? Why can't you support my ideas?"

He glanced at her, then pounded his fists onto the steering wheel. "Christ, Gina, why do you have to be so difficult? Don't you want to play with the big boys?"

"Terry, not everyone wants mass-produced jewelry. I think there is a market for specialty designs, one-of-a-kind things. People who shop in the boutiques aren't looking for things they can get anywhere."

Terry flashed her a scornful expression, rolled his eyes, then looked away. He was quiet for several minutes before he turned to her again. "Well, you can forget about us going up to the lake this weekend.

Before we go any further with this relationship, I think you need to do an attitude evaluation."

"Attitude evaluation?"

"Yeah." He straightened up in his seat. "Decide if you want to be in this relationship or not. This isn't working for me, so you can forget about a romantic weekend."

"But I've already cleared it with the store so I could be off."

He pulled his lips into a tight line. "Well, that's too bad. I don't feel like being romantic with you right now."

"Oh, Terry," she sighed, and touched his arm. "I'm sorry you feel that way, but you know, it's hard to be around you sometimes. I'm always afraid you'll go off on me about some little thing I do or say that you take the wrong way."

"Oh, so it's all my fault?"

"I'm not saying that. It's both of us. When you get demanding and critical, it makes me nervous. It's hard to relax around you when I feel like that."

Terry jerked his arm away. "Then maybe we should just forget the whole thing, Gina. I have a lot to offer. Lots of women would be thrilled to be with me. I have a great job, I make good money, drive a nice car, and have a lot of friends."

Yeah, a lot of other selfish, immature, crude guys just like you.

"Did you say something?" he asked.

"No, I was just thinking…"

"Well, think about this, Gina. You're not getting any younger. This is probably your last chance to find someone to settle down with."

"Terry, I'm only twenty-four years old!"

"Like I said, this is probably your last chance." Terry parked in front of Gina's house and sat with a sullen scowl across his face. He did not offer to get out of his seat and walk with her to her door.

From her memory, Gina's grandmother whispered, "Never let anyone make you feel like anything less." She grabbed her keys and turned to him.

"I've been thinking, Terry. Maybe you're right."

"Yeah?"

"Yeah."

He reached for her.

She pulled away. "Yeah, I think you're right about this not working."

She opened the car door, scrambled out quickly, and walked to her front door. As she jammed the key into the lock she heard the sound of Terry gunning the engine and backing out of the parking spot. He drove away with the squealing of his tires on the pavement.

Gina didn't look back. As soon as she was safely inside, she pushed the door shut and locked it, then stood in the hallway for a few moments. Completely drained, she walked into the living room and flopped down on the sofa. Tears burned her eyes and she tightened her hands into fists. *Damn him! This was supposed to be such a good evening, and a special weekend coming up. How had things gone so wrong in such a short amount of time?*

And yet, unbidden and unexpected, a sense of relief swept through her as if a weight had suddenly lifted.

I can breathe again.

Chapter 2

Spring—Phoenix

ALMOST TWO YEARS LATER, when Gina recalled the cruel things Terry had said, it still hurt. Even though she dated since that time, nothing seemed to work out. She wondered if she could ever completely trust any of the men she dated.

Instead, she focused on her career.

Her other interest was a townhouse she bought, located at the base of a mountain preserve.

Gina loved the quiet and the sunlight that streamed in from both the front and rear windows. Everything about the house seemed light and airy. She installed white stone tile on the entire ground floor and hung gauzy white curtains in the windows. To this, she added comfortable, overstuffed sofas, and filled the shelves with all kinds of books. A wall unit housed her stereo and television and a growing collection of DVDs and CDs. She hung artwork she liked on the walls.

She remodeled the back porch into an extension of the living room, connected with white French doors. The result was a modern, open living room with a floorplan that allowed visitors to move around with ease. Her house became a place where friends loved to gather.

A guest bedroom was converted into a combination office and work area.

Upstairs, Gina expressed her feminine side by ordering a lovely old-fashioned brass bed, *"the most beautiful bed I ever saw."* She draped it with a white, lacy dust ruffle and comforter, together with several oversized pillows.

For bedroom furniture, she chose beautiful pine antique reproductions: armoire, double dresser, and night tables. The bedroom was unusually large, so she added an arm chair in a corner, complete with a reading lamp. Several white rugs scattered across the oak hardwood floor. The finished bedroom looked like a photo in a decorating magazine. The antique brass bed and pine furniture balanced each other, giving the room an updated old-fashioned look.

Outside, a balcony stretched the entire length of the bedroom. The view of the mountains behind the house was spectacular. At night, she could stand on the balcony and look up at the stars. When it rained, she could watch the rain as it refreshed the trees and desert vegetation below.

"Very appealing," Lynn commented when everything was completed. "The downstairs is modern. Geometrical but inviting, and the bedroom is charmingly old-fashioned. I think it's very romantic."

"Kind of like me," Gina said. "A mix of modern and traditional."

Lynn smirked. "I really love the bed. It sets the whole room off, kind of like one of those private get-away places for couples. You could have a lot of fun in here."

"Maybe, but I designed it for me to enjoy. After all, I'll probably be living here the rest of my life."

"Hopefully you won't be in here all by yourself forever. I'd like to see you find someone one of these days. Maybe the reason why things haven't worked out so far is because you haven't met the right one yet."

"Maybe."

* * *

Shortly after she moved into her townhouse, Gina's parents visited. To her surprise, they liked the house and expressed admiration for the way she had furnished it.

The next morning, her father said, "Gina, come sit with me. Let's talk." He patted a place beside him on the sofa and Gina joined him.

"I'm glad it's just the two of us here now," he began. "I want to talk with you while your mother is out at the supermarket."

Gina waited.

"There's another reason why we wanted to make this trip… I had a mild heart attack a few months ago."

Gina's head jerked up. "What? Why didn't anyone tell me?"

"I didn't want to alarm you. Besides, it wasn't serious. I didn't want you to worry."

"How could I not worry? You're my father."

"Yes, and I've been doing some thinking about that. A heart attack does that to a man—makes you think. I realize I probably haven't been much of a father to you; always away and always busy. But it doesn't mean I wasn't interested in you or didn't love you. I have always loved you. I've watched as you grew up and made your way into the world and I'm very proud of you."

He said nothing more for several moments, then added, "I can see now that I didn't have a good way of showing it. I suppose I'm like many successful men; we have an idea that our job is to provide for our wives and children. It doesn't occur to us that our children need more than financial support. They also need our presence in their lives. I realize now I have been lacking in that area. I'm sorry, Gina. I never meant to hurt you."

Gina's mouth dropped open.

"And, I know your mother has been rough on you. But try to understand her perspective. She was a girl from a small farming town, but she completely re-invented herself to be what she thought I needed. A perfect corporate executive wife. She learned how to talk, how to walk, how to dress, how to entertain. Everything she thought was expected of her. Kind of like the old days, when girls went to finishing school.

"She wanted to raise you with those standards, too, so you would grow up already knowing how to fit into society. So she came down hard on you. But believe it or not, she did it for love, and for her hopes that you would not have to learn the hard way, like she did. She wanted you to have the tools you would need to have the kind of happy life we've had.

"And we have been happy, Gina. I was her knight in shining armor, and she has been my queen. I married her because I fell in love with her. We've traveled the world together and had a remarkable life. We have been partners in everything. We wanted that for you, too, but somehow it didn't come across that way. I know she wanted perfection, but it's because she wanted your life to be perfect."

Wow. What a revelation. Gina expelled a long breath as the truth of this testament vibrated through her.

Tears stung her eyes and ran down her face. "But Daddy, she was mean to me."

Gently, her father put his arms around her. "Please know that I was away so much that I didn't realize at the time. But I can tell because of the way the two of you interact now. I think you're afraid of her. Please don't be. Try to understand she thought she was helping you. Try to forgive her."

Gina cried into his shoulder. "Thanks for telling me this, Daddy. I love you," she sobbed.

"I love you too, my little girl."

For the rest of the week Gina saw a side of her parents she had never known. They had many animated conversations and took walks along the mountain trails behind the house. By the time her parents ended their visit, Gina experienced a connection with them she had never thought possible. Her feelings about herself shifted as a result. *Maybe I belong in this family after all.*

Even after her parents left, Gina felt a difference in how she saw her place in the world. Some of her old fears about not being good enough began to fade, and she gazed out at the world with a new vision.

But two weeks after the visit, her mother called with the news that her father had suffered another heart attack. This time, he did not survive.

Numbed with shock, Gina observed all the funeral rituals in a state of disbelief, helping her mother make arrangements and filling out the necessary paperwork. After the funeral, she stayed behind to watch as the casket was lowered into the ground and covered. A simple marker was placed over the grave to mark it until the engraved tombstone could be installed.

Gina walked around the site, her thoughts in turmoil. Is this all there was? The grave seemed so small. With all the things her father had accomplished in his lifetime, was this all that was left?

And yet, Gina knew better. Seeds planted by a person in this life would still sprout after the person had departed. She thought back to the recent visit and the day she and her father had talked. What a gift he had bestowed upon her with his words! A blessing. Had he known he would die soon? Was that the reason he had come to see her; to impart this gift to her while he still could? She knew this was something she would ponder the rest of her life.

* * *

Back at work, Gina focused on being a good manager, and was promoted again, to oversee two departments. She spent a lot of time with her salespeople and tried to be fair to everyone without playing favorites. As a result, she had an extremely loyal staff, and was well-liked throughout the store, even back in Shipping and Receiving, where rock music usually boomed from the speakers. Quite a change from the usual "elevator music" piped into the rest of the store. One day a song caught her attention. She stopped to listen.

A young man working in the area noticed her. "You like that?"

"Yeah, I do. I've never heard this before. Who is it?"

"My band."

"Really? You're good. What's the name of your group?"

"Personality Disorder. We play around town sometimes, when we can get a gig."

"Well, I'm impressed." Gina gazed up into hazel-blue eyes in an earnest face, framed with sandy hair. "I didn't know we had talent like this working here."

"Thanks. I'm Graham, by the way. I'm taking some classes at the community college, and working on my music. I just work here to pay the bills. Not bad for a nineteen-year old kid, huh?"

"Not at all. It's nice to meet you, Graham. I'm Gina."

"Yeah, I know." He smiled. "Word is that you're one of the best managers in this place. One of the nicest, anyway."

"Well, thank you."

"So, you like rock music? You should come and hear us play sometime. It'd be nice to look out and see some friendly faces in the audience."

"I guess it would. Just let me know and I'll try to come. You know where my office is, don't you? Drop in anytime."

"Deal."

Over the next few months, as Gina and Graham talked about bands and songs, they became friends. She could always count on him to make her laugh, even on stressful days.

"Hey, Gina!" he greeted her one morning. "My band is playing this week. Why don't you come to hear us?"

"Really? Where and when?"

Graham's smile lit up his face. "We're playing Thursday night at a place called The Garage. It's kind of a dump, but still, it gives musicians starting out a place to play. You know how it is. First, we play at home, in the garage, and then we play at The Garage." He laughed at his own joke.

Gina laughed, too. "Okay, you've got yourself a deal. I'll get Lynn to go with me. I think she has to work late that night, but if we leave right after the store closes, we should be there by the time the place heats up."

"Cool." Graham's eyes crinkled with a smile.

"Great. I'll see you then."

* * *

Thursday night after work, Gina drove with Lynn to the address Graham had provided.

"I can't believe you dragged me out to this place," Lynn drawled as the club came into view. "Look at this dump—it's not exactly in the best part of town."

"Don't worry," Gina soothed. "I think a lot of people from the store are coming tonight, so we won't be alone. It should be safe enough."

Lynn made a kind of snorting noise and stared out the window.

Gina found a place to park next to several other cars in a vacant lot. People were heading toward the club. From the casual way they were dressed, Gina was glad she had changed to a pair of jeans.

The door opened to admit the group in front of them. A loud thumping beat came from inside. The door closed again, but she could still hear thumping, now muffled, seeping out into the otherwise quiet night.

A very heavy-set man sat next to the door. *Get a load of all those tattoos! What kind of place is this?*

"Could I see some identification please?" the tattooed man said.

"You're carding me? You've got to be joking," Gina scoffed. Beside her, she noticed Lynn rolling her eyes.

"Yep. I have to ask everybody," the man said, folding his oversized arms across his chest.

Gina and Lynn opened their purses and dragged out their drivers licenses

The man scanned both licenses, then returned them and opened the door for them. As they walked inside, the volume of the music engulfed them like a tidal wave.

"Good Lord, Gina, I can't believe you talked me into coming to this place!" Lynn shouted over the noise and rolled her eyes. "Did you see that? They've got a bouncer who looks like a fugitive from a chain gang!"

"I'm sure his mother loves him very much," Gina said, and watched a slow smile spread across Lynn's face, despite her complaints.

They found a table near the front so they could be sure that Graham would see them when he came on stage. A waitress appeared, and soon they were relaxing with a couple of drinks.

Gina scanned the crowd, noticing people chatting together. Some were couples, some were in groups, and others strolled around the floor. Sporadic greetings were called out across the crowd.

"Look at this place, Lynn! There must be at least fifty people in here! Where did they all come from?"

Lynn surveyed the crowd. "I don't know. I guess everybody is just into the music."

The band that had been playing finished their set. They began to break down their equipment so the next band could set up. Graham wandered across the stage, connecting wires and bringing in instruments.

Gina studied the interior of the club. Everything looked gloomy and gritty, dark as a cave. Even the ceiling was black. There was a bar on one side of the room, and a tiny stage in front. In the back were several pool tables. The room was hazy with smoke. Posters of various groups hung on the walls. Kind of grungy, but the place was crowded and no one seemed to be bothered by the dark atmosphere.

Gina's thoughts slowly focused. A lot of these people seemed to know each other. No one was bothering anyone else, not even the biker group seated at one of the tables. Everyone looked as if they were simply enjoying a pleasant evening out. How normal.

In a sudden flash of insight, she saw what was missing from her life. She had grown so focused on her career that she had made no recent attempts to get out or make efforts to meet other people. Her world had become too narrow, with work her only interest. True, it offered a kind of buffer against getting hurt in a relationship, but she had carried it to the point where she had made herself unavailable and untouchable. Now she felt marooned. It was true that she was successful. Sales were up and her staff loved her. Suddenly that wasn't enough. She realized she had let her job expand into all of her time, keeping her so busy there was no time to get lonely.

For the first time as she examined her life from a perspective outside herself, she realized that her position would continue, even without her. If she suddenly was not there, the company would simply find a replacement for her and business would go on as usual.

And, while she had been so busy with her career, time had slipped away. Now, she could not think of anything she had gained that was worth trading so much time for. She took a long swallow of her drink as she considered this. *Something will have to change. I deserve a life, too. I have a right to be happy.*

Graham's band finished setting up their equipment. Graham walked to the center of the stage, wearing jeans with holes in the knees and a faded denim shirt. He took the microphone from its stand and waved to the audience. With his guitar slung behind his back, he yelled into the microphone, "Welcome to The Garage! We're Personality Disorder, and we want to rock you!"

The band crashed into the introduction of their first song, and Graham leaned forward with a scream. He dropped to one knee, stood up again and shook out his hair. All that hair he had been forced to tie back at work flew up through the air, ending in long curls around his shoulders.

He squinted in concentration as he sang, then threw his head forward and bent over his guitar. A heavy instrumental section followed, then more hair flying through the air as he returned to the microphone and finished his song.

A thundering of "Whoo-hoos!" whistles, and clapping erupted from the audience.

"Thank you!" Graham said, smiling. "We're glad you came to see us tonight... and now, here's a new number we just wrote." They started their second song.

Gina found herself tapping her feet in time. *They're pretty good. Graham really takes this stuff seriously. Even though he works hard at the store every day, he obviously has another completely different, separate life outside. Why haven't I ever thought about that possibility? I've talked a lot about my jewelry for years, yet after all this time, that's all it is—just talk.*

"All this time and nothing to show for it," she said out loud. She thought again about Graham. He really believed in his music, and he was actively doing something about it. She remembered how he had told her about all the hours he spent practicing, and now, here he was, center stage, performing his finished arrangements.

She sat back and listened. Some of the songs she remembered from the day she had first heard Graham's CD out on the receiving dock, but most of them were new to her. The number of songs and differences between them were a testament to the amount of time and effort that had been spent in their creation.

In comparison, she thought about the amount of time she had seriously spent designing her jewelry. Not much, she realized. Just doing it on a once-in-a-while basis would not generate the kind of results she dreamed of. If she was ever really going to do anything with it, she needed to get started. She sighed, thinking of the hours she spent on her job. Somehow, she must begin to re-claim her own identity from the corporate-molded personality she had become.

She sat quietly, ignoring her drink, wanting to keep her head clear so all these new thoughts could bounce around in her brain for a while.

Graham's face dripped with sweat. She remembered what he had told her about how hot it could get up on stage, under the lights, but he didn't seem to mind. He was clutching the microphone as if he was afraid it would be taken away from him, living in his world of lights and sounds.

He looks so happy. He's doing something he really loves. No wonder he's always in such a good mood at the store—he knows he has a place in a different world, so he doesn't let all the craziness upset him. Lucky.

I could have the same kind of thing if I want, but I've got to make the effort and be willing to pay my dues, just like he has.

With that resolution made, she relaxed and enjoyed the rest of Graham's show.

The band received a standing ovation. They bowed and thanked the audience again and explained that they had to clear the stage for the next band to set up.

Gina watched the members of the band break down their equipment and wiring. She was fascinated, never having thought of how much equipment was required to do a show like this. One load followed another out a door behind the stage where a parked truck waited.

On their way out, she and Lynn bumped into Graham, who was just coming back in. He beamed at them. "Hey, thanks for coming to see us!"

"You didn't think I would actually show up, did you?" Gina asked.

He grinned. "Well, maybe. You're managers, and I'm just a lowly peon in the store."

"We loved it! See you tomorrow."

"And, Graham?" Gina called back over her shoulder, "Let me know when you're playing again."

"Deal!" he yelled.

All the way home, Gina thought about her new decision, excited at the thought of a life outside the store. The possibilities seemed unlimited.

* * *

In the morning, Graham appeared in Gina's office just before the store opened.

"So, you really liked it?"

"Yeah. I did. I think you have a lot of potential."

Nothing could have made Graham happier, from the look on his face. "Thank you." He gave her a hug. "It really means a lot to me that you came, and if you liked the songs, then I'm over the moon."

She grinned. "Well, I think you're good. You should keep going with this."

"I plan to. I need to keep practicing, and I want to learn the sound board, too. I've got an application in with House of Rock. If I get the job there, I'll get to work with bands coming through on tours. I know I can learn a lot from that."

"Wow! House of Rock is a big step up from the Garage," Gina exclaimed. "They have nationally-known bands come in there."

"International bands, too. They've had several British groups in there, and some dudes from Australia. I'm hoping they'll have some of the new groups from Japan, too."

"Japan? They have rock bands in Japan?"

"Are you serious? Some of the Japanese groups are the best in the world. They're part of the J-Rock Revolution."

"What's that?"

"Japanese Rock Revolution. Kind of turning the rock world on its head. They're just so good. All of them. Still Japanese, but expressing things in a completely new way. I loved EZO and Loudness. And X Japan. They were really into visual kei. Their shows are just unbelievable. Brilliant."

"What's visual kei?"

"Like Kabuki theatre on steroids and electrified with a wall of sound," Graham said and winked.

Noticing the questioning look on Gina's face, he explained. "Visual spectacle, intense fullness of sound. The total package all pulled together, but under that, solid musical skill. So cool. I wish I could see X Japan in concert, but they sell out stadiums of fifty, sixty thousand people in a matter of hours. They're far too big to ever play at House of Rock."

Graham sighed. "But hopefully, other groups will play there. And, if I'm working at the club, I'd get to meet all of them."

"That'd be a great experience for you. I hope you get the job!"

"Thanks," Graham said. "I've got a pretty good shot at it since I know one of the guys who works there. He said he'd put in a good word for me with the manager."

They were interrupted by a page for Graham to report to the receiving area.

"Well, gotta go," he said. "It's showtime!"

Gina gave him a quick hug. "You'd better get moving. It might just be the Weasel out there."

Graham's smile faded. "I hope not. I'm in a good mood so far today!" He grinned at her and rushed out the door. "Later!"

* * *

A few weeks later, Gina walked back to Receiving to check on a damaged carton. Graham was there, talking with another department manager. He waved and shouted, "Wait for me in the office. I'll be there in a minute."

Gina nodded, walked into the office and sat down next to a desk smothered with paperwork, stacks of files, and a newspaper open to the entertainment section. A circle was drawn around a write-up about a band called Moonstorm that was scheduled to play in a place called Club Malibu in a few weeks. Gina picked up the paper to take a closer look.

Graham wandered in, carrying a tool box and more papers.

"Hey, almost done. Gotta find a packing slip." He set the tool box down, rummaged through a stack of documents, and pulled one out.

"Oh, hey, check this out." Graham pointed to the circled area on the page. "I always like to keep up with who's coming into town. Remember I told you about some of the groups from Japan, and how good they are? One of them is coming here soon. I hear they do a really great show. You might want to go and see what you think." He headed out the door.

Gina glanced at the article again. The thought of a band from Japan was intriguing. Somehow, she couldn't imagine a Japanese group playing rock music. Maybe she would take Graham's advice and go.

The following week, she noticed another article about the same band in a monthly magazine that covered local events.

She was interested. Curious. Gina decided to go, and asked Lynn to accompany her, explaining that she didn't want to go by herself, and besides, Lynn was always good company.

"Oh, all right," Lynn reluctantly agreed.

Chapter 3

Spring—Phoenix

DARKNESS DESCENDED ON THE ROOM, then came the announcement, "And now, Club Malibu is pleased to present Moonstorm!" Foggy smoke swirled around the stage as the lights slowly came up.

From somewhere within the inky darkness, blue spotlights suddenly erupted, illuminating four figures emerging from the fog. The band opened with a powerful, unusual set of chords, then launched immediately into their first song.

The impact was total. The entire crowd became attentive. All talking ceased as everyone leaned forward to hear. The music was loud, so loud that the floor was vibrating underfoot, but no one objected.

Gina stood with her mouth open, transfixed. She had not expected to be impressed, thinking it would probably be the same kind of music she was used to, but this was different. Different and better. The songs varied in styles and intensities, the rhythms shifting, even within a song. Instead of a usual basic beat, this group used a more sophisticated style, with syncopation that made the flow of music more interesting. Interspaced with heavy, dramatic chords and vocals were sections of beautiful, haunting solo guitar work. The interplay of heavy and soft tones reminded her of the light and shade she admired in great works of art, or nights spent in the desert, staying awake to watch a silvery moon floating within a sea of clouds, light chasing shadow across the sky.

Her eyes wandered to the lead guitarist, who had first caught her attention because he was the tallest of the four. He stood almost solemnly, as though absorbed in some private world, part of the group, yet apart from the rest. He had the blackest hair she had ever seen, gleaming under the lights, defiantly long and yet very masculine. He was tall and slender, almost willowy, but he moved with a kind of controlled grace that indicated a powerful energy. His shirt was worn partially unbuttoned, Cossack style, belted low over his hips, giving his movements a fluid quality. Black pants fitted tightly over long, slim legs and black leather boots. A silver chain glinted around his neck. She imagined the chain might be a gift from a girlfriend, then wondered why such a thought bothered her.

Get a grip, she told herself, but she was unable to look away. She watched in fascination as his fingers moved up and down the neck of his guitar, creating sounds new to her. Some kind of energy seemed to radiate out from him in a way she couldn't explain.

He has an almost perfect face, she thought, now staring at him; a face with large dark eyes that seemed to take in everything as he calmly glanced around the room. She knew she was too far back in the crowd for him to see her, but when his eyes swept past the place where she stood, she drew in her breath sharply. *Wow. He is really sexy.* Those smoldering eyes, that hair! The way he moved! The sweet look of concentration on his face ... But, did he always look so serious?

She saw him nod to another member of the group in some kind of communication, then suddenly, he smiled—a flash of white against midnight hair. A tremor like an electric shock rippled through her and she wondered if she could still breathe.

Damn! She frowned. What was wrong with her anyway? Why did she suddenly feel confused? What was it about him that attracted her so much?

The rest of the show passed in a blur. All she could be sure of was that she liked everything she saw and heard. The members of the band blended together well, moving from one song right into the next. When they finished their set, they were brought back by enthusiastic applause for two encores.

"Come on, let's go," Lynn said, nudging her. "We can get out of the parking lot before the rush if we hurry."

As they drove away from the club, Gina asked, "Lynn, isn't there a music store in the mall?"

"Yeah, I think so. Why?"

"Do you think they would have this band's CD?"

"I don't know. You could call and ask."

"I'll do it tomorrow. I want to get that CD."

"Really? I didn't know you were into heavy metal music."

"You'd be surprised what kind of stuff I like. Don't you remember all the CDs I have at home?"

"Oh, yeah, that's right," Lynn agreed. "I forgot. It's been a while since you listened to much of that, hasn't it?"

"Yes, and maybe that's been a mistake," Gina said softly, almost to herself. "Maybe that's what's wrong with my life. I think maybe I need to get up and dance more, and listen to music more, and the hell with everything. Maybe it's time to make some changes."

"Maybe…" Lynn said.

Gina was no longer listening to Lynn. Music from the group she had just heard filled her head with refrain after refrain, the handsome face of the guitarist filled her vision, and she suddenly realized it had been a long time since she had felt so completely *alive*. All her senses were tingling.

At lunch the following day, she walked to the music shop in the mall and purchased the band's CD. She hurried back to her office and carefully unwrapped the package, then put it into her little CD player.

The disk sounded just as good as she remembered. A few of the songs were instantly recognizable as some she had heard the night before. Others were unfamiliar to her, but they were all good. While she worked on her reports, she played the CD over several times, listening carefully to the words and again enjoying the beautiful guitar solos. She found herself wondering what the lead guitarist was doing at this moment. Was he in some other city, getting ready to do another show tonight? She was fascinated and could not stop thinking about him.

* * *

After work, Gina met Lynn for a quick dinner at a local burger restaurant. As they ate, they discussed plans for an upcoming sales event.

Gina's thoughts wandered to the night before and she changed the subject.

"Lynn, what did you think of the band last night? Do you think they were good?"

"Oh, yeah!" Lynn exclaimed enthusiastically, waving part of her sandwich in the air. "I couldn't believe they were Japanese! I didn't know they had music like that over there, but they were great. I'd go to see them again, wouldn't you?"

"Yes I would," Gina agreed. "Did you notice the guitarist? What did you think about him?"

"Oh, him," Lynn said. "Yeah, I noticed him. I never saw hair like that in all my life, not in real life, anyway. Really black. And long."

"Yeah, I know," Gina sighed. "But didn't you think he was kind of good looking?"

"Well, I suppose so," Lynn began, then suddenly noticing the turn the conversation had taken, turned to glare at Gina and asked, "Why? What are you up to?"

"Oh, nothing…"

"Oh, come on now!" Lynn snorted. "I know you better than that! I can tell you're up to something, so out with it!"

Gina thought for a moment, then announced, "Lynn, I'm going to tell you something I want to keep just between us, because it sounds a little crazy. I like that group, and I like the guitarist. I'm going to find out everything I can about them, and the next time I get a chance to see them, I'm going." She hesitated, noticing Lynn's upraised eyebrows, then added, "And when I do, I'm going to find some way to meet him. Do you hear what I'm saying?"

"Oh my Lord!" Lynn exclaimed, laughing. "I hear you all right, but I just can't believe it. You've got to be kidding! A guitar player in a band? You're a management professional! What on earth would you want with a guy in a band?"

"Why not him? I like him, I like the songs he writes, and I think he's got talent."

"Hey, I'm not knocking it," Lynn drawled. "I'm just surprised. I didn't think you would be interested in somebody like that is all."

"Well, I'm not sure if I'm interested in him or not, but I am interested in meeting him. I read the liner notes on the CD and it looks like he wrote most of the songs. I've been listening to them, and somehow I feel a kind of connection –like maybe we've had some of the same experiences in life. I know it sounds crazy…" her voice trailed off. "But I think we might have a lot in common."

"Well then, go for it!" Lynn said, laughing. "Let me know if you ever get to meet him."

"Agreed!" Gina said, and they raised their glasses in a toast.

* * *

Later that week, Graham came to her office carrying parts for a new display fixture.

He stopped and cocked his head toward Gina's CD player. "Hey, that's Moonstorm! I love that group!"

"You know that band?"

"Of course. They're part of the J-Rock Revolution. Great group! They were just here in town but I didn't get to see the show. Too bad, those guys rock!"

"Yeah, I know. I went to see them."

"You did?"

"Yeah, I went with Lynn."

"Oh, man, I wish I'd known you were going! I would have gone with you. So, how was the show?"

"Loved it—got the CD the day after the show and I've been playing it ever since."

"Awesome! Maybe they'll come back to do another show."

"I sure hope so…"

Graham peered at her and grinned. "Oh, ho. You want to meet them."

"Oh, God, is it that obvious?"

Graham laughed. "Hey relax. I won't say a word. I'd like to meet them too."

"I really liked the guitar player... he was... incredible."

"Oh, that would be Taro. He's the leader of the group."

"You know their names?"

"Oh, yeah. I know a lot about them. So, you like Taro?"

"Well," she blushed. "He's... he's really interesting looking. And talented."

"Yeah, he is." Graham winked. "Hey, our secret, okay?"

"Thanks, Graham. You're the best!"

"I know... hey, where do you want these boxes? You want me to take them out behind the counter so the girls can start putting it together?"

"That would be great. Let me come out there with you so I can set up the rack. Maybe we can get the whole grouping put out before the Weasel makes his next round."

"Good idea. I hate it when he whines."

"I know. He really is a pain."

* * *

One afternoon in late June Gina hurried to the receiving dock to respond to a page from Graham. Since Graham had started working at the House of Rock, she didn't see him as much as before, and always looked forward to catching up with him.

"Oh, hey, Gina!" he called when she appeared. "I just paged you!"

"That's why I'm here. What's up? Is there a problem with something?"

"No, not at all." He winked and glanced around to be sure they were alone before he continued.

"I've got some information for you. You remember that Japanese band we talked about, Moonstorm?"

"Yeah... what..."

"Well, guess what? I just found out they're booked to play at House of Rock in a couple of weeks. And since I'm working there now, I'll get to work with them, doing the sound checks and helping backstage during the show. Are you still interested in meeting that dude who plays guitar for them?"

"Oh!" she was shocked. "Well, yes."

"Okay. Just be sure to be there that night and I'll try to introduce you. What do you say to that?"

Gina hesitated.

"Something wrong?" Graham inquired.

"Well… I don't know… Will he think I'm some kind of groupie?"

Graham looked startled. "Nah, no way," he shrugged. "You don't look like the type."

"The type? What do you mean?"

"Oh, you know."

"Not really."

"I think you do. The type that looks like they just want to get a guy into bed because he's in a band. I see it all the time."

"You do?"

"Oh, yeah." Graham grinned. "Don't forget, I'm in a band, too. It's pretty easy to spot the girls who just want to party."

"Oh. So, has that happened to you?"

"Sure. I'm sure Taro has had his share of that kind of attention, too. Guys in bands know the look. There are some of them who go for it, sure. Some are famous for it. But there are plenty of others who don't."

Gina blushed.

"Hey, don't worry," Graham soothed. "From everything I've heard about Taro, I think he's very careful. You never hear anything about wild parties or anything like that about him. He's serious about his music. You can tell from his songs."

"What do you mean about him being careful?"

"Well, I think he is very aware that he is a foreigner here. He doesn't want to do anything to embarrass himself or his country—nothing to make Japan look bad. He's very humble and polite."

Gina said nothing, and Graham added, "Gina, don't worry. I'll be there with you just in case he turns out to be a jerk. But I think he's probably all right."

"Thanks, Graham. I appreciate it. I guess I'm more nervous about this than I would have thought. I've never met anyone like that before."

"I know. It's pretty obvious. But don't worry. I'm sure he'll be nice, so at least you can say you met him."

Gina grinned. "Yeah, you're right. Thanks, Graham. I'll owe you one!"

"Hey, you don't owe me. You're the nicest person in this place." He sighed. "Maybe you can put in a good word for me when it's time for my review."

"Oh, Graham, you can count on it."

"Our secret, okay? I won't say anything to anybody. The big boss probably wouldn't approve."

"Yeah, no kidding. Besides, what does a Weasel know about rock and roll?"

"Not much," Graham laughed. "That's probably why he's so uptight all the time."

"You might be right about that," she agreed, and they laughed together.

* * *

After the show, Graham greeted her warmly and hurried her backstage. She could see the members of the band talking together by one of the back corners. Someone was taking pictures, and it looked like a reporter asking questions. She could hear laughter mixed in with language unfamiliar to her. Overall, the mood seemed friendly.

"Wait here a minute," Graham told her. "That's him, over there. I'll go get him."

"Okay, Graham. Thanks."

He winked at her and strode off.

Gina noticed her hands were shaking. Quickly, she turned around and pulled a mirror from her purse so she could do a last-minute check of her hair and makeup. *What's wrong with me? Why do I feel so nervous? It's not like this is the end of the world or something. I won't ever see him again after tonight, anyway. Get a grip!*

The mirror reflected a pair of smoky green eyes outlined in black, with thick black lashes above a clear complexion, high cheekbones and full lips shiny with gloss. Under the club lights, her hair gleamed like white gold, short and spiked a little on top.

Not bad, she had to admit to herself, and bent to replace the mirror in her purse. When she spun back around, she crashed against a figure in a black leather coat who hadn't been there before.

A hand reached out to steady her and she looked up at Taro.

"Wow, you're really tall!" she blurted out, then blushed completely red.

Oh my God! What an idiotic thing to say.

The expression on Taro's face shifted from amusement to irritation.

"I'm sorry," she tried again... "I don't usually fall on people like that. I am sorry..." she trailed off, not knowing what else to say. Her face burned with embarrassment.

"No, she doesn't," Graham interjected, and laughed.

They both turned to look at him.

"Sorry, but I think it's funny," Graham explained. He motioned toward Gina. "Taro, this is Gina, one of my bosses where I work. Gina, this is Taro."

The look of irritation disappeared as Taro raised his eyebrows. His eyes were soft now. Curious. Open.

He reached for her hand and held it for a moment. "It's nice to meet you," he said, with just a hint of a smile.

His fingers were warm.

He released her hand but stood where he was and tilted his head toward her. "So, did you like our show?"

"Yes, very much."

Up close, he was definitely taller than she had expected, and his hair was even longer than she remembered, thick and glossy. She liked that.

His face was interesting, with well-balanced features and large, dark, wide-set eyes that seemed to notice everything. He had a smooth, light complexion, but under his eyes, shadows hinted at fatigue. His lips were well-shaped, hinting of a smile.

Gina realized she was staring. *I like his face—everything about it. And his lips. Very kissable.*

When he spoke, his voice was soft, a rich medium tone, and her impression was that his words were carefully chosen, polite.

"Your English is very good," she ventured shyly, meaning it as a compliment.

The reaction she got was not quite what she expected. A flicker of irritation crossed his face, and suddenly, he looked tired. He sighed. "We are not all short, funny-talking little people running around with cameras, you know."

He folded his arms across his chest and his mouth pulled into a tight line.

Oh, my God! Could this get any more awkward? I meant well, but I think I've insulted him and possibly hurt his feelings to boot.

She stared at him, dumbfounded. Was she imagining it, or did he look hurt? The look on his face was serious, yet somehow despite her best intentions, she had to laugh.

At this, he laughed, too. His arms dropped to his sides and he smiled at her.

"You're right," she agreed. "And we are not always so rude. I am sorry if I said something wrong. I didn't mean to… I did want to meet you, but I just didn't know what to say. I really do like your music…"

"That's right," Graham cut in. "She's cool. We listen to your stuff all the time."

"Really?" Taro said. He tilted his head toward her and his eyes swept from her face down her figure and back up to meet her eyes.

Someone called his name and he glanced around. The other members of the band were moving out through the back door. Through the open doorway, a tour bus was parked behind the club.

He turned back to them. "It's too bad we have to leave now because we could all go out for a drink."

"Hey, man, that would be great!" Graham remarked.

"But we have a show in California tomorrow."

Okay, Gina, this is your chance. For once in your life, go for it! What have you got to lose?

She smiled up at him, and teased, "Well, the next time you're in town, why don't you come to my house for dinner? It would give me a chance to make up for my bad manners."

He blinked in surprise and stared at her. His lips turned up at the corners in a slight smile. "Maybe I will."

She pulled a piece of paper from her purse and wrote on it. "Here is my name and my phone number," she said and gave him the paper.

"Thank you for this," he said, regarding her curiously but politely, almost bowing. He looked at the paper, back at her, then folded it and put it in his pocket.

He smiled and took her hand again for a moment. "I really have to leave now. It was good to meet you," he said, his voice very low. He released her hand, and turned toward the back door, to the bus. She watched him walk up the steps. He paused to look back and raised his hand in a wave, then stepped through the opening. The bus door closed and she could hear the engine revving up.

"Wow!" Graham whistled. "That was too cool. I think he liked you."

"You don't think I blew it?"

"No. I think he's interested. He certainly won't forget you anytime soon."

"Really?"

"Oh, yeah. He was totally checking you out. I wouldn't be surprised if he doesn't call you when he's back here again."

"You're not just saying that because we work together, are you?"

"No. I'm a guy. I know these things, okay?"

"Oh." She blushed. "Hey, Graham, let's keep this just between us, okay? Don't say anything to anyone at the store."

"Sure. Why would I say anything to that bunch of idiots? You're about the only one I like in that place anyway."

"Thanks, Graham. You're the best!"

"And don't you forget it!" he laughed. "Don't forget to keep coming to hear my band play, too."

"It's a promise."

Chapter 4

"HERE WE ARE AGAIN," Lynn grumbled before the managers' meeting the next morning. "Another boring meeting. This will be the high point of my day, so you know what kind of day I've been having."

"Ouch!" Gina winced.

Lynn rolled her eyes at Gina. "I can't wait to hear the words of enlightenment the Weasel has for us this time." She settled back into her chair with an expression of supreme boredom.

"I'm in a good mood," Gina chirped. "I've got some news."

"Spill," Lynn drawled. "Anything would be better than waiting for this meeting to start."

"Lynn, do you remember my telling you that there was somebody I wanted to meet, if his band ever came back to town?"

"Yeah," Lynn said, suddenly alert. "And?"

"Well, they were back last night, at that place where Graham works now."

"So?" Lynn pressed, leaning toward her.

"I went to see them. After the show Graham introduced us."

"You're kidding."

"No."

"Okay, so you met him. What was he like?"

"Really nice. Polite. Gorgeous. Really long hair."

Lynn rolled her eyes again. "Oh, Gina, you're crazy." But she smiled.

"But wait, there's more!" Gina teased. "I invited him to dinner the next time he's in town. And, I gave him my phone number."

Lynn lurched forward and stared. "What? Are you serious? What did he say?"

"He said 'thank you'."

"Okay," Lynn sighed. "So, what do you think will happen now? You don't really expect to hear from him, do you?"

"Who knows? Graham said he thought so. He said the guy was totally checking me out."

"Oh, my Lord, Gina, you're nuts," Lynn laughed. "It'll be interesting to see what happens, if anything. At least you'll have something else to think about besides this place."

"No kidding. Thank God."

"And, he's a lot better looking than the Weasel," Lynn smirked.

Gina glanced down, hoping Lynn wouldn't notice her face redden. Her thoughts were suddenly far away, remembering Taro's smile when she gave him the paper with her phone number, and the feel of his warm hand around hers. She wondered where he was at this moment.

* * *

Two months later, Gina flopped down on her bed, deciding what to wear for her date with Jason. He would be picking her up soon to attend a surprise birthday party for one of his friends.

"What do you think, Cheddar?"

Cheddar raised her fuzzy orange head and stared into Gina's eyes for a moment and yawned.

"Yeah, you're right," Gina sighed, stroking Cheddar's furry little body. "It really doesn't matter. You can tell, can't you? I don't know why I even agreed to go out with him again. I'm just not interested. There's really no point in continuing to see him."

Cheddar yawned again. She stretched out her front paws and settled into Gina's lap. Gina scratched behind her ears and was rewarded with the sound of purring. She thought back to when Cheddar first came to stay.

Terry had called her again about six months after they broke up. He said he missed her. Gina agreed to meet him for dinner, thinking that everyone deserved a second chance. The dinner went well, and they went out a few times, but it wasn't long before he was once again criticizing and 'advising' her about almost everything. They quickly separated again. This time, Gina resolved to stay away from him for good.

After several months, she had almost forgotten about him when she received an urgent call. Terry told her he had found 'the love of his life' and was now planning to relocate to Alaska with her. He asked if Gina could take his pet cat because it would be too much trouble to take her with him. When Gina hesitated, Terry said, "Well, if you don't take her, I'll just have to put her in the pound."

She sighed. *More attempted manipulation.*

Gina knew the pound was almost certainly a death sentence. The facility did the best they could with limited staff and budget, and far too many unwanted animals. She thought about Cheddar, who had always been friendly to her. *That poor cat. She didn't do anything wrong, but suddenly she's an inconvenience, and he just wants to throw her away.* "All right, Terry, I'll take her."

Terry insisted that he needed to bring her over immediately. Gina agreed. If she had to see him again, she might as well get it over with as fast as possible. Besides, she wanted to get Cheddar in a safe place in case he changed his mind and just drove straight to the pound.

About an hour later, Terry showed up at her door with Cheddar in a carrier, a bag of kitty litter, and food. Gina noticed it was the cheapest brand of cat food on the market. Terry set the carrier down on the living room floor. He opened the door and Cheddar appeared, glancing around, looking nervous and frightened.

"Well, she looks like she'll make herself right at home here," Terry implied, flashing one of his fake smiles. *Like a politician.* "Thanks for taking her, Gina. I'd stay, but I have an appointment, so…"

"Of course," Gina soothed. "Don't worry about it, Terry. She'll be fine."

Terry looked relieved and left soon thereafter. Gina locked the door after him.

Thank God. What a miserable excuse for a human being! She shuddered. *I'm glad he's moving away. After today I will never have to see him again.*

"Hello, Cheddar," she cooed in a soft voice. "Welcome to your new home."

Cheddar crouched with her back raised and hissed. She hissed a few more times and began to creep slowly around the room.

She's terrified. She just got evicted from the only home she's ever known, stuffed in a carrier, and dumped off in a strange place. Poor cat.

That night after Gina went to bed, she heard Cheddar meowing loudly downstairs. She went down to the kitchen to make sure there was enough food and water and called softly to the cat, opening a small can of food and placing some of it on a plate. Cheddar stared at Gina but did not come any closer.

"You poor thing," Gina soothed in a soft voice. "Don't worry, Cheddar. You're safe here."

Cheddar growled and hissed.

"I'm going back to bed, so you can eat when you want," Gina offered. She left Cheddar in the kitchen and returned upstairs.

In the morning, the canned cat food was gone, but Cheddar maintained her distance. She lashed her tail from side to side, her eyes wide with suspicion.

It took months before Cheddar relaxed. Gina noticed that if she reached out with her hand, Cheddar would shrink away. She wondered if Terry had hit her. *He must have. Why else would she be so afraid all the time?*

One morning, Cheddar must have decided that everything would be all right, because she meowed, abruptly climbed into Gina's lap, looked up and purred. After that day, Cheddar followed Gina everywhere, even jumping up on the bed at night, snuggling close to Gina's side.

Gina focused back to the present. What to wear for tonight? She stood up and turned to her closet. After deciding not to wear a dress, she settled on a simple pair of jeans and a Hawaiian print shirt.

The doorbell rang. Gina sighed. "Well, he's here. I'll see you later, Cheddar."

* * *

"I want to talk with you about something, Gina," Jason brought up as he drove her home. "Is it okay if I come in for a few minutes?"

"Sure."

They went inside and sat together on the sofa. Gina waited.

Jason got right to the point. "Gina, you know I really like you a lot. I enjoy going out with you, and I think you're a very special lady. I'd like to see how you feel about taking our relationship to the next level."

"What?" Gina was stunned. She enjoyed Jason's company when they went to movies or out for dinner, and he had kissed her goodnight a few times, but she had been careful never to let anything happen beyond that. She wasn't sure why at first, but finally realized that she just didn't feel any chemistry with him. *No sparks. Nada. Zip.*

Now, he was apparently asking how she felt about becoming a couple.

"Gina, I want you to think about the possibility of us. I know I'm not making a fortune as a high school football coach, but my family is very well off. We could have a comfortable life, if you want."

Oh, my God. How do I get out of this without hurting his feelings?

"Jason, this is really sweet, and I'm flattered. I think you're really a great guy and you're a lot of fun to be with, but I don't think I'm the right one for you. I think of you as a friend. A very good friend. I enjoy going out with you, but we're not really interested in the same things. You're a nice Southern gentleman, and I love that about you, but I don't really like football or team sports like that, and football is pretty much your whole world. It's what you talk about all the time, and all you want to see on television. Even tonight at the party, most of the talk was about football. Past victories, predictions for the future, the players, the Superbowl, that kind of thing."

"Oh, Gina, I can talk about other things, too…"

"Please, Jason, let me finish. I don't want to change you. I like you the way you are. It's wonderful, how you help the kids in your school. You're a good role model. But I don't like the pressure put on kids to be on the team, and the chance of serious injuries from all the physical confrontations. And, I'm concerned that the percentage of kids to really make it in the game is so small. If kids spend all their time in school thinking about football instead of learning other things, I don't think they will come out well prepared for the future.

"Wow, Gina, that's pretty extreme. That's really how you feel?"

"Yes, Jason. That doesn't mean there is anything wrong with you. Not at all. You're good at what you do. The kids love you. You were a big star in your Georgia Tech days, and that's great. But I think you need to find someone who is interested in sports like you. Maybe a cheerleader coach, or someone else who shares your interests. It's not that I don't like sports, but what I like is individual stuff, like hiking or scuba diving or going out on a kayak, something like that. I'm also interested in the arts and music. I love to read and go to plays and foreign films. In all the time I've known you, we have never done anything like that."

"Well, I can change. We can do some of those things."

"Jason, if you were really interested in those things, we would have already done some of them by now. It just isn't something that interests you as much as football."

She stopped and took a deep breath. "Jason, like I said, I like you the way you are. You're a wonderful guy. And I don't want you to change for me, or for me to change for you. The feeling of wanting to come together and share, and grow together has to come naturally, or it just doesn't work. I'm not the right girl for you. The perfect one is out there somewhere, waiting for you to find her."

Jason sat quietly, then smiled and glanced at her again. "Well, you certainly have given me a lot to consider. I appreciate your being honest with me, but I'm still hoping I can change your mind."

Unexpectedly, he reached for her, clutched her to his chest, and kissed her. Gina was shocked to feel his tongue push deep into her mouth and all over her lips. *Yuck!* He held her in a viselike grip so tight she couldn't breathe and pushed her head back with the force of his kiss. *Oh, double yuck! He's grossing me out!*

She managed to push away. Jason sat there looking pleased with himself. "So now, you have a little something more to think about," he said with a smile.

Oh, my God, he actually thinks that was a good kiss. He thinks he's good at it. I think I want to throw up.

"Wow, Jason. That was some kiss. It definitely gives me something more to think about," she said, rising from the sofa. "But I need to be in the store extra early tomorrow for a meeting, so I need to say goodnight for now." She smiled at him, but inside, she felt revolted.

Jason took the cue. He stood up too, and they walked to the door.

Just before he left, he turned back. "Promise me you'll think about it," he said with a wink.

"I promise. Goodnight, Jason."

As soon as the door was locked, Gina ran up the stairs to the bathroom and washed her mouth out with Listerine. She thought she could still taste him, so she rinsed twice.

She stared at her reflection in the mirror and addressed the image of the flustered, irritated woman who stared back. *Oh yeah, I'll think about it. And what I think is no way! Not even if hell freezes over!*

She stomped into her bedroom. "You don't know what I had to put up with tonight, Cheddar. I absolutely guarantee this is the last time I go out with Jason! If he calls again, I will always have an excuse. I will never put myself in that situation again. Ugh!"

Cheddar blinked her eyes.

"You knew, didn't you, you smart little cat? You knew. I noticed you never wanted to be close to him when he was here. I should have paid attention. You're a psychic cat. And I'm lucky to have you in my life." She nuzzled Cheddar's ears.

Cheddar purred.

Gina sighed. "At least I tried. I tried to find someone. Jason just wasn't the right one. I wonder if there will ever be someone for me. Someone that wants me as much as I want him. Someone who is interesting and fascinating and wonderful. What do you think, Cheddar? Maybe someone like Taro? Is there a chance for me?"

Cheddar blinked her eyes again and tucked her front paws under her body.

For the next several weeks, Gina stayed at the store even later than usual, trying to avoid any contact with Jason. He called every day. At home, she let the phone go to voicemail. If Jason called her at the store, she always told him she was in a meeting or in the middle of some project and couldn't talk.

Late one night, just as she was getting ready for bed, the telephone rang.

"Damn!" she snapped. "Why doesn't he take a hint?" Feeling extremely irritated, she stomped into her bedroom. *I'm tired of having to deal with this. Maybe it's better to just confront him and put an end to it.*

She yanked the receiver up. "Hello," she said, noticing that her irritation showed in her voice.

After a long moment of silence, she was ready to hang up, thinking it must be a prank call or wrong number, but she froze when she heard a voice in slightly accented English say, "So sorry to call this late. I am calling for Gina. Is this Gina?"

Oh, my God! Could this be Taro? "Yes, yes, this is Gina," she gushed. Her heartbeat hammered in her ears. "I was getting ready to go to bed."

"Oh, I am sorry," he said again.

"No, it's okay."

"This is Taro. I met you about two months ago. A friend of yours introduced us after the show. Do you remember me?"

Mr. sexy eyes and kissable mouth? How could I forget?

"Yes, I do," Gina said, trying to sound friendly and cheerful. "How are you?"

He did not answer her question. Instead, he said, "We will be back in Phoenix in a few weeks. I wanted to ask if you still want me to come for dinner at your house."

"Yes, of course. I would like that."

She could hear him expel a long breath on the line. "I would like that, too," he said.

Was it her imagination, or did he sound happy? She knew she would lose sleep tonight wondering about it. "Do you know exactly when you will be here?"

"Not yet, but soon. I'll call you back when I know. Is that okay?"

"Yes, that would be fine."

There was a pause before he spoke again. "Okay. That sounds good. I will call you again soon."

"Okay."

"Well, goodnight, then," he said.

"Goodnight. Thank you for calling."

She heard the phone line go dead as he hung up. "Oh, my God!" she squealed. "Taro called! He called! That beautiful, sexy man just called me, and he wants to come here, to my house! Did you hear that, Cheddar? Taro called me!"

Cheddar opened one eye and winked.

* * *

"Hey Lynn, you'll never believe who I got a call from last night," Gina teased at lunch the next day.

Lynn paused in mid-sandwich. "Who?"

Gina sat in silence and smiled.

Lynn raised her eyebrows. "Well?"

"Someone I never thought I'd hear from." She gestured an imitation of long hair. "Someone I met about two months ago."

Lynn stared. "You've got to be kidding me."

"No."

Lynn's mouth dropped open.

"Really," Gina continued. "He called last night. He actually asked if I remembered him. Can you imagine?"

"No, I can't. So, what did he say?"

"He was sweet. Very humble. He said they'll be coming back through here on their way back east. Then he asked if I still wanted him to come for dinner."

Lynn sat gawking in silence for a moment and rolled her eyes. "Oh, Gina, I guess I'm not surprised. You're so crazy I should expect anything from you. So, when is he going to be here?"

Gina lowered her voice. "I'm not completely sure. Sometime in the next couple of weeks. He said he would call again to let me know."

She winked at Lynn. "Maybe if I'm lucky, he'll be here when I have my next three-day time off."

Lynn tried not to laugh. "So, what do you think you can do with him for three days?"

"Well, you never know!" Gina laughed, and blushed.

Lynn rolled her eyes again. "Oh, Gina…" she said, but she was laughing. Suddenly her smile was gone. "Oh, crap. The Weasel is on his way in. We'd better get looking serious. We'll talk about this later, okay?"

Chapter 5

Early September—Phoenix

THE DOORBELL RANG. "Try not to be nervous," Gina commanded herself. She glanced out the window by her front door.

Taro was standing on her front step, looking back at someone in a van. When Gina opened the door, he turned, gave her a quick glance, and waved the van away.

"I'll be back to pick you up in time for the show!" the driver shouted.

Taro nodded and gave a 'thumbs up' sign, then turned back to Gina, tilting his head toward her. "Hi."

She drank in the sight of him, absorbing all the details. Black leather pants and a dark red shirt belted low, just above his hips. Over that, a long black leather coat. His hair fell below his shoulders, thick and black.

She realized she was staring and struggled to remember the phrase she had been practicing.

"*Irashaimasse. Kore wa watashi no uchi desu. Dozo…*"

(*Welcome. This is my house. Please come in…*)

He raised his eyebrows in surprise, bowed slightly, and stepped inside.

She hung up his coat, and returned to find him still standing where she had left him, just inside the front door.

"*Dozo,*" she repeated, smiling and gesturing to the living room. "Please come in and sit down"

He followed her and sat down on the sofa, watching her in silence.

After an awkward pause, she asked, "I'm going to make some margaritas. Would you like one?" and rose to fix one for both of them when he nodded.

She dumped ice cubes and drink mix into the blender and flicked it on.

This isn't going well at all. I've finally got him over here, and he isn't saying anything. What do I do now?

She returned with the drinks and settled into a chair opposite him. He sipped his drink slowly, but she noticed his eyes slowly sweeping the room, absorbing everything.

I wonder what's going on in his head. My God, he has beautiful eyes.

She took a huge gulp of her drink.

"How did you learn to say 'welcome to my house'? Are you interested to learn Japanese?" He tilted his head toward her.

She blushed. "It's something I've always been interested in. Really. In school we studied about Japan when I was in fifth grade. Ever since then, I've always wanted to go there." She looked down at her feet. *I should have come up with something better than that, even if it was the truth. That probably sounded pretty stupid.*

If he thought it sounded stupid, he gave no indication. He regarded her in interested silence for a time.

Was she boring him? Was he just being polite? She couldn't tell.

"How did you learn to say that?"

"I asked a teacher," she admitted, staring down at the floor.

This is awful! I've probably made a real ass out of myself. What should I say now?

"I, uh, need to start the dinner," she stammered, rising quickly from her chair, wanting to escape to the familiar comfort of her kitchen. "Why don't you look through the CDs and pick out some music to put on?" She waved her hand at a box in the corner and fled the room.

* * *

Taro stood up as she left, an amused smile on his face. He didn't understand why she was acting so embarrassed. He was impressed that she had tried to learn something of his language. Most Americans never even attempted it.

He scanned the room and located the box of CDs she had mentioned. He rummaged around for a while, noticing that she had

CDs of everything from classical music to ethnic dances and all kinds of rock. What she didn't have was the typical collection of pop singers that crammed the airwaves on most radio stations. He smiled at this, already liking her more. He selected a disk and put it into the stereo, and the room filled with the soft, lush sounds of a classical selection.

He walked to the kitchen to see what she was doing and leaned back into the door frame.

She glanced up to see him standing there and blushed.

"For dinner, we're having fish," she announced. "And some vegetables, and other things. I know Japanese people eat a lot of fish, so I hope this will be okay."

"Since I have been here, I have become used to eating American food. I like it." Then, seeing the dismay on her face, he added, "But, I still like fish too. You're right about that."

She looked relieved, and it occurred to him how nervous she must be, inviting a stranger from another country into her house and attempting to cook for him.

He watched as she wrapped the fish in foil to steam, and fluttered around with various pots and pans. She must have gone to a great deal of trouble to plan this, he thought. And, he had to admit, it had been a very long time since anybody had done anything special just for him. He felt himself warming up to her.

He held out his hand with her glass. "You have been so busy you didn't finish your drink."

"Oh, I almost forgot it," she laughed, brushing the hair back from her face.

He handed the glass to her, and their fingers touched.

Wow. Did he feel that, too? Like an electric shock just zapped through me.

They stared at each other for a moment.

She finished her food preparations and they returned to the living room to wait for the dinner to cook.

Armed with her second drink, and feeling bolder, she inquired, "I'm curious about how you got into music. I know American music is popular in Japan, but making it a career must be quite a break from your traditions."

He nodded. "We have a lot of traditions in Japan about how people should live." He sighed and lit a cigarette, inhaling deeply. "It is not easy to be different."

She nodded, encouraging him to continue.

"I wanted my music to be a way to get away from all that. If I went into a normal business, my life would be much more regulated. Music gave me a different opportunity. It is not what my parents planned for me, but they finally understood."

"Did they want you to take music lessons?"

He smiled. "Yes. I started piano lessons when I was very young, but I had no idea then that music would become so important to me. I learned both classical Japanese and Western music. It was hard at first. Western music has eight note octaves, but Eastern music has five, seven, or twelve tone scales. That's why they sound so different. I had to practice all the time. I hated it. My mother sat with me and made me practice."

"Poor little kid!" she teased. "You must have been too busy to have much fun."

He frowned. "In Japan, a student is not supposed to have fun. It is a time for learning. Everyone is serious about preparing for entry exams to the universities. Only students with the best scores are admitted."

"Really?" She sat back and compared this to her own experience.

"It must seem strange to you," he softened a little, "but it really isn't so bad. All the other kids are doing the same thing. There isn't much time to get into trouble."

He stopped and looked around for an ashtray.

"Oh!" She quickly rose and ran back to the kitchen, returning with a small dish. "I'm sorry. I don't smoke," she explained as she set it on the table next to him.

He raised his eyebrows at this and put out the cigarette. "Thank you."

"Were you a good student?" she eased back into their conversation.

"Yes," he admitted. "A serious student. Science was my favorite subject, but I got good grades in everything. I was quiet and shy back then, and my teachers all liked me. My parents were hoping for a good university. I got into one of the best ones."

She smiled. *I knew he was smart.*

"Did you take music lessons while you were in school?"

"Of course. I played the piano for years, but I practiced for hundreds of years!" He chuckled at his little joke. "Actually, I got to be pretty good, and enjoyed it. Even now, I like to play piano."

"Really—like what?"

"Beethoven piano sonatas. I also like Chopin."

Gina stared at him. Who could have guessed this? She was astonished. She could not imagine any of the musicians she had seen in symphonies playing rock music… but she had never spoken with a professional musician before. "So, what Chopin composition do you like best?"

"Waltz in C sharp minor," he answered without hesitation. "My mother really likes it when I play that."

"Well, I must say I'm impressed," she admitted. "I would not have thought that someone who plays heavy metal would be interested in classical music."

He laughed. "They have more in common that you would think. They both have heavy tones mixed with elements of lightness, and they both can be really loud and complex. Lots of drama."

"Sounds kind of like a Wagner opera," she suggested. "I don't know if you are familiar with the Ring operas, but they are so dramatic, so full of sound and fury, so… so total in their presentation. It takes a huge theatre to hold all the sounds."

He nodded. "When there was a Wagner festival in Japan, I went to all the shows, and I agree with you. Those performances really blew me away."

They stared at each other for a few moments.

He picked up the conversation again. "Of course, when I was still a kid, I didn't know about all that yet. Japanese people do not usually talk about themselves, so a lot of the music was not very personal." He stopped and lit another cigarette.

"But then I listened to some of my uncle's old records and tapes. He had everything. Elvis, the Beatles, Jimi Hendrix, Led Zeppelin and KISS. I went to his house all the time and listened to everything he had. It really opened me up and I started to change. I remember when I first heard the Beatles' song 'Eleanor Rigby'. It was one of my uncle's favorites. That song really touched me. It was so sad. I realized there must be thousands of people like that in the world, all wanting to belong somewhere, and not knowing how. It made me see that music could say something about the world I saw and how I felt about it."

"Yes, I remember that song, too. My father liked it. And I agree. Sometimes one person's story in a song can touch the whole world. Some feelings are universal."

"That's exactly what I mean."

She sat in silence, not knowing what to say. The level of sensitivity he had exhibited was a surprise.

He was quiet for a few moments before he continued. "I really loved my uncle's Jimi Hendrix records. So original! And what he did with sound – so cool! And Led Zeppelin. I could hear that they had fun with their music. I mean, they just said whatever they wanted. Like in 'Whole Lotta Love'. They actually said 'I'm…'" He stopped abruptly as the implications of the song suddenly registered. He hesitated and his voice trailed off. "Well, you know," he said shyly. He shifted uncomfortably and reached for another cigarette.

She blushed and stared down at her feet. Of course she remembered the famous lyrics. She wondered what it would be like to make love to him and what it would feel like to have him inside her, way down inside. She could feel his eyes on her as her face burned with embarrassment. Was he aware of the effect of his presence on her?

There was an awkward silence, but neither of them rushed to fill the empty space.

After a moment he continued.

"That song shocked me! I just couldn't believe it. I mean, until then, no one had ever said such a thing in a song before. But they were serious musicians, world famous, and I liked the freedom it represented." He exhaled a long breath of smoke. "Now almost all rock music is about personal stuff."

Taro shook his head and laughed before he continued, "I was glad then for all the years of practice because I could copy the songs I liked. I could figure out the notes and how the songs were put together. I played guitar and keyboard, and got together with some other boys. We played together, and we would hang out and smoke and try to look cool. You know." He laughed again. "I started to grow my hair longer. We all did. My parents didn't like that. They made me keep it cut until I left for the university."

Oh yeah, the long hair is totally hot.

I wanted to be as good as musicians from other groups, like X-Japan and EZO and Loudness." He exhaled another long breath of smoke.

"All of that must have been really hard for your parents to accept," she suggested.

"*Hai.*" He sighed. "My life has not been an easy choice. Sometimes I feel torn. I want to be close to Japan and my family, and yet I feel I belong here. It was very hard for my parents to accept the idea of my coming to America. They were afraid I would never return to Japan. No one in my family has ever done such a thing before."

He thought for a moment before continuing. "And, I have changed by living here. Now, when I go home to Japan, I look at everything there with different eyes. I miss the freedom here. Sometimes I don't feel that I belong there anymore…" he trailed off.

"I think I understand how you feel," Gina suggested.

"Really?" He looked surprised.

She explained. "When I was about fourteen years old, I visited my old home, where my family used to live. Everything looked different and felt different. All my friends had made other friends. Their lives had gone on without me. I didn't quite fit in anymore. It hurt a lot."

He nodded in understanding.

They sat without speaking for a few minutes.

"I think maybe I talk too much," he apologized.

"No, not at all. All of this is really interesting. But, I think dinner is ready now. Why don't we eat?"

He stood, and as he followed her to the table, she was very aware of his eyes watching her as she walked.

She served the dinner and poured some wine. While they ate, he told her some of the funny things that had happened to him since coming to America. The mood was warm and casual. It seemed to her that he was trying to be amusing, but she sensed that there was something else he wanted to say but didn't, for some reason.

After dinner, they returned to the living room. At her invitation, Taro put another CD into the stereo, then sat down in a chair across from her.

"Your dinner was very good," he said carefully, trying to choose the right words. "Everything was perfect. Thank you for inviting me. I have enjoyed talking with you."

"I have enjoyed talking with you, too," she said. "I'm glad you came." She wondered if he was getting ready to leave now. *Please, not yet.*

There was another period of silence. *What is he thinking about?*

"It doesn't bother you that I'm Japanese?" he asked after some hesitation.

"No," she answered in a defiant whisper. *So that was it. That must be what he had been thinking about before, when he seemed to be holding something back.* She smiled at him, wondering where things would go from here.

Taro seemed to consider this, then he crossed the room and sat beside her on the sofa. He bent forward, resting his elbows on his knees, his head in his hands. When he spoke, his voice was so soft it was as if he was talking to himself.

"I know I am not a typical American," he said, slowly reaching for the right words. "I want to be here, but why should I not be proud of being Japanese, too? My culture has given me a different understanding of life that I want to share through my music."

Gina turned to study his serious expression. His words had unlocked a door into his experience, like a curtain being raised to reveal a totally new world different from anything she had known before. He had not moved from where he sat, so near they were almost touching. He was so close that she could feel his warm breath on her face when he spoke.

They sat without talking, yet the space between them was alive with the energy of sending and receiving signals.

Gradually, the mood lightened, and he smiled at her. Something pulled on her heart that was almost painful.

A flash of panic made her want to run, into the safe, familiar routine of her life. *Life without him. Dull. Lifeless. Boring. No. I don't want him out of my life—not yet, anyway. There's something about him that won't let me turn away.*

Realizing that she was staring down at the floor, she glanced up into his eyes. He smiled again, a soft, gentle smile. His intelligent eyes seemed to be looking through her as if he understood clearly the differing thoughts at war within her. He sat very still, and his calmness eventually calmed her, too. They sat this way for a long time, saying nothing, understanding everything.

When she rose to refill their glasses, she felt shaken.

What is it about this guy? He's smart, there's no doubt about that, but he's also really nice. But it's more than that. He's so ... tuned in. He seems to know exactly what I feel. That's a little scary. I wonder if he knows how attractive I think he is. I've been fantasizing about him for months, imagining all kinds of things, wondering what it would be like to hold him, to love him, wanting to for some reason I can't explain. I bet he knows all that, yet he has only been polite. Not many American guys would have been so nice and not tried to get me into bed already.

She returned with more wine, and rejoined him on the sofa. She knew there was not much time left before he would have to leave, and that would be that.

Who knows, maybe someday we will meet again.

Trying to wrap up this encounter on a positive note, she ventured, "I hope you have a chance to see more of America while you're here."

He nodded. "We live in New York, but I have seen some of America from the tour bus. When we were driving across to California we stopped to see the Grand Canyon. I liked it."

"Really?"

"Yes. I wanted to see something of America besides just cities."

She brightened. "That's good, but there's a lot more to see besides just the Grand Canyon. It's too bad you didn't have time to see some other areas that are not so well known. Some of the most interesting places are kind of off the map."

"Like what?"

"Some of the land up on the Rez. It's definitely worth the time to go up there."

"You mean some of the Indian lands?" He moved closer and now regarded her with outright interest. "I would really like to see that."

"You would? Why?"

"Because many Japanese people believe we are related to American Indians. Some kind of cultural connection."

"Well, I'm driving up to northern Arizona tomorrow. Up to the Reservation and maybe some slot canyons." Then without thinking, she added, "You can come along with me if you want."

"Really? The tour bus is getting repairs, so we aren't going anywhere tomorrow. You are serious? You are inviting me to go up there with you?"

"Uh, sure, if you want to." Her thoughts were suddenly in a turmoil. Who would have thought she would have provoked such a reaction? She realized he was waiting for her to say something. "I was planning to drive up there early in the morning. I've already made arrangements to rent a cabin. Nothing fancy at all. Very rustic. I want to hike. You know, just get out and walk."

"What's rustic?"

"Just a little wooden cabin. Nothing like this," she gestured around the room. "Very small, maybe just a fireplace."

Taro leaned closer, his eyes dancing. He smiled. "Yes. I would like that."

She was stunned. He couldn't possibly be serious, could he? To him, she said, "Well, okay, if you really want to."

A horn blared from outside.

He stood up. "It's my ride to the show. I have to go." But then he continued with, "What time in the morning?"

"I wanted to leave around 6 AM, to get out of town before the traffic gets bad." She could not believe the turn this conversation had taken. Surely, he was just being polite. He couldn't possibly have any intention of really going along with this crazy idea. Or did he?

"Okay." He stood up and walked with her to the door.

"Thank you again for dinner," he said very formally. He took her hands in his. "But I have to go now."

"I know," she said. "The show must go on, right?"

He opened the door and waved to the waiting car outside. Just before he stepped out onto the porch, he turned and looked at her one more time, then he was gone.

Suddenly, everything in the house seemed too quiet, almost as though he had never been there.

She was left alone with her thoughts.

What a crazy night this was! How had she managed to get into a situation like this, she asked herself as she cleaned up the dishes and got ready for bed. Still, it was a nice evening. A nice fantasy. He had been so very polite, and probably was just making conversation by saying he was interested in something she liked. Nothing more than that. He probably had invitations from women all the time. He must be used to fancy hotels and traveling all over, and getting a lot of attention. Why would he possibly be interested in going along on some off-the-beaten-track adventure with someone he had just met?

It was difficult for her to sleep. She kept going over everything that had happened, over and over, and it was hard not to smile. What a beautiful man he was! And those eyes! It was an impossible situation, but tonight would be a really nice memory.

Chapter 6

Northern Arizona—the Navajo Reservation

MORNING CAME WITH A JOLT when Gina's alarm clock went off. *Time to jump in the shower and get ready.*

Her mind kept wandering off, to the absurd notion that Taro might have been serious about wanting to come along. She shook her head. Nah, no way. Last night wasn't real. She didn't want to think about it. *A dream.*

But she did want to think about it.

Okay, so on the road I'll think about it.

"I'd better hurry so I can beat the traffic," she told herself as she zipped up a small overnight bag. She was reaching for a jacket when the doorbell rang. She froze.

It can't be. It's 6 AM.

She ran downstairs and peeked out the window. Behind a dark human shape standing on her porch, a taxi was driving away. The bell rang again. She pulled the door open and Taro stepped inside, briskly rubbing his arms from the cold.

He smiled. "Good morning. Are you ready to go?"

She stared at him. He had on a pair of jeans and a sweater. Evidence of a collar peeked out underneath. A leather jacket was tucked under his arm.

He looks like a regular guy. Except for the long hair. And the boots.

He grinned and gestured to the sweater. "I got this from one of the sound guys. Is it okay?"

"Uh, yeah. It can get cold in the high desert. I can't believe you really want to do this," she added.

"Why not? I told you so. Maybe some kind of culture connection." He wiggled his eyebrows.

I can't believe this!

"I need to go and get my bag," she stuttered. She left him for a moment and ran upstairs, returning with her overnight bag and hiking boots.

"Oh, I almost forgot—I made coffee." She walked into the kitchen and brought out a thermos, two cups, and bottles of water.

"Do you want anything to eat before we go?" she asked.

"No, I'm not hungry. We can get breakfast somewhere on the way, can't we?"

"Sure."

"Then, is that everything?"

"Yes."

He grinned. "Then let's go!" He picked up her bags and they walked out. He glanced around as she locked the door. "Which one is your car?"

"Right here," She pointed to her Jeep.

"This? This is what you drive? A Jeep Wrangler?"

"Why not? I love it. What did you expect?"

"I'm not sure. Not this. I thought most girls drive pretty little cars."

"On the east coast, maybe. Besides, I'm not most girls."

He shook his head at this and smiled. "No, you're not."

"I'm a western woman! This is the wild west. Some of the roads we have out here would tear up a pretty little car. I wanted something that would handle anything."

"Well, I'm from Tokyo, and now I live in New York, so I only know what people in big cities drive. I've always wanted to try one of these." He walked around to take a closer look. "I think it's cool that you drive one. Does it have gears and a clutch?"

"Yeah, it's a five-speed. It's also a four-by-four, so I can drive on any kind of terrain and in all kinds of weather."

"I like it," he admitted, clearly impressed.

"Well, city boy, in that case, get in and let's go. *Banzai!*"

He bit back a laugh and bent to pick up her things.

Taro put her bags behind the seat with the thermos and climbed in. He watched while she started the engine, shifted into reverse, and backed out of the parking spot. She paused a moment, shifted gears, and they bolted forward into blackness.

They drove past miles of sleeping residential areas and malls until they were out of the city. It was still dark when they turned onto the Beeline Highway. She put in the clutch, shifted gears again, and they rushed ahead into more darkness, climbing up toward the mountains.

They shared the coffee from the thermos and later stopped at a MacDonald's for breakfast as the sun was just beginning to warm the horizon.

She was curious. "Weren't you up really late last night after the show?"

"Oh, yeah, the usual. But then I went back to the hotel to sleep."

"But how…?" she started to ask.

"Wake-up call," he confided with a serene smile.

She absorbed all of this in silence, but she smiled. *He actually planned ahead for this.*

The highway meandered through pine forests and mountains. Another road forked north. Trees faded behind them as the road swooped downhill to flatter, drier land. They crossed I-40 and continued north through country that became more remote and unearthly as they drove.

* * *

Taro remained in the Jeep while Gina checked into the motel office. Flustered by the reality of the situation she now found herself in, she inquired about sleeping arrangements in the room. *That's what comes from doing something impulsive. Why didn't I think about this before? Well, obviously because I never thought I'd have to deal with it for real. Now here I am, with him. What does he expect will happen? Oh my God! What the hell was I thinking?*

She was advised that the cabin contained two single beds. *Thank God. I won't have to deal with that situation.* Still, her heart beat faster just thinking about it.

She decided to be low-key and nonchalant, in case he said anything, and returned to the Jeep with the key.

She drove to the cabin and parked, then unlocked the door and they went in. The two beds were there, with a small lamp table between them and extra blankets folded at the foot. Other than that, there was a fireplace, a small bathroom, and nothing else. The cabin was extremely tiny.

Taro said nothing as he brought in their things from the Jeep. After a few minutes, they left again to drive to the canyon.

She parked in an area next to the trail head, where they got out and began the descent into the canyon. Walls of sheer rock extended to the canyon floor, in bands of color. How old this land was! Evidence of past geological disturbances was everywhere, with layers of rock twisted into strange lines. In places, cliffs resembled faces with watchful eyes, where caves had formed over the years.

Gina bent down to take a closer look at some stones next to the path.

She reached out and picked up a rock, then showed it to Taro. "Look at these colors!" She smiled and put it into her pocket, then stood with her hands on her hips, searching the landscape.

"What are you doing?" he asked.

"Looking for rocks for my jewelry."

"You make jewelry? How?"

"I shape pretty stones into hearts and drill holes for a chain. Then I polish them until they're smooth so you can see the layers of colors. Each one is different. I sell my jewelry in some of the boutiques over in Scottsdale that cater to wealthy tourists."

The expression on his face showed interest and curiosity. "Don't you need a lot of equipment for that?"

She gazed up at him and pushed her visor back. "Sometimes. It depends on what kind of jewelry you're making. For this, I use a Dremel drill and a rock polisher." She fished the rock from her pocket and held it out to him.

Taro took a step toward her. He took the rock from her hand and examined it. "How long have you been doing this?"

"Oh, a long time."

"So, you make jewelry to sell, and work at the store, too?"

"Yeah. Aren't you impressed? She joked.

"Actually, I am." He placed the rock back in her hand. "What else do you know how to do?"

"Oh... lots of things..." and she cast him a sidewise smirk.

Taro raised his eyebrows at this and smiled.

What the hell did I say that for? Her face began to burn with a blush, so she turned and started back down the path. He followed, catching up to her so they could walk side by side.

They continued to the bottom of the canyon in silence. The path twisted in unexpected turns that sometimes almost doubled back on itself. In places the trail led through narrow passes between boulders, and they had to walk single file. After some time, they stopped and sat on a large outcropping of rock to rest.

Taro noticed a small rock and picked it up.

"For you."

"Oh! Thank you."

He leaned closer. "Do you think it would make a good heart for your collection?"

"Yeah. I like the colors. And look, there's some sparkle in it, too. This is a really nice one." *Wow. He actually listened and paid attention to what I said.*

He placed the rock in her hands, and when his warm fingers touched hers, a sensation like an electric current tingled through her.

"Ready to go?" he asked.

"Sure."

They continued walking. She pulled Taro's rock out of her pocket to look at it again and smiled.

At the very bottom of the canyon, they entered a natural stone tunnel. When they emerged from the far end, tinkling sounds jingled from tiny bells on the sheep that wandered in small enclosures kept by Navajo families. Other than the bells and sounds made by the wind, there was a peaceful silence. It was another world, like stepping onto a different planet.

They crossed the dry streambed running through the canyon, to an area where ancient cliff dwellings seemed to float high above the canyon floor. Taro stared in awe, absorbing everything.

"It's almost a religious experience, isn't it?" she commented. He nodded silently.

* * *

Dark clouds bloomed in the sky by the time they got back to the cabin. They were both hungry after all the hiking.

They made a fire before walking to a local restaurant so the cabin would be warm upon their return.

Their waiter was a shy teenager who was very polite and smiled constantly. Gina glanced around and noticed quite a few Native American men with hair as long as Taro. Other than their waiter, no one paid any attention to them. It was nice to fit in, she thought, and felt herself relax.

While they waited for their food, Taro regarded her with curiosity. "Tell me, how did you get the idea to make jewelry?"

"When I was a little girl, I used to go hiking a lot, and picked up rocks from everywhere. I wanted to do something with them so they wouldn't be hidden away in a box. I asked the neighbor next door about it. He showed me how to use a drill to shape and polish them. So I started making necklaces for some of my friends.

"How old were you?"

"About ten or eleven."

He looked surprised. "So, then what?"

"I really liked making things. Sometimes I combined stones with shells and beads. Later I got the idea to make jewelry to sell. I thought if I got good enough, I could start my own business.

"I would like to see some of the things you made. What was the first thing you sold?"

"You'll laugh, but one day I decided to take some rocks out of our driveway to see what I could do with them. You know, to practice. They weren't very pretty, but I shaped them into squares and drilled holes through them and strung them together. After I polished them, they were a soft grey color with just a little shine. I made a necklace out of those rocks."

"With rocks out of your driveway? Really?"

"Yes. And I sold it to a lady for a hundred dollars. She loved it, and said it was just the thing to go with some of her business suits."

Taro stared at her, laughing. "That's great! So, after that, you decided to make some more?"

"Yeah, I did. I sold every piece I made. No one ever guessed they were wearing something out of the family driveway." She laughed and took a sip of her drink.

"Later, I got the idea to shape some of them into hearts. So, I ended up with a collection I called 'Hearts of the Earth'. Every piece was from rocks I found. People love them because each one is unique."

"I think that's really interesting." He smiled.

I wonder if he has any idea how he makes me feel when he flashes that smile. Like it's hard for me to catch my breath.

She smiled back, trying to regain her focus. "Now I'm working on some new ideas with silver stars and crystal beads. I call it my "Starstruck" collection. And I'm thinking about doing something with silver and leather."

"You have a lot of creative ideas," he said earnestly, leaning closer. Does the store know you are doing this?"

"No. And I want to keep it that way."

"I completely understand."

"Do you?"

"Yeah. It's important to have something no one else can take from you."

"Like your music, your creativity. No one can own that but you."

"Exactly."

They sat quietly for a few moments staring at each other.

Outside the restaurant, cold monsoon rains pelted them on the way back. By the time they reached the cabin, they were completely soaked and chilled, but they were laughing and making jokes about trying to talk through chattering teeth.

They spread blankets onto the floor in front of the fire and tunneled in underneath. Still chilled from the cold, they clung to each other until the warmth from the fire filled the room.

He sat up, pulling her up with him. She realized he was still holding her and that her arms were around him too. Neither of them moved, but sat quietly looking at one another for a long time.

"We should get out of these wet clothes," he finally said.

When she said nothing, he added, "We can stay in these blankets until our clothes dry."

He began to pull his sweater off. She turned away quickly, but she could hear that he was getting the shirt off, too, then the boots, thrown one at a time beside the fire. Then she heard the clinking of his belt buckle and wiggling sounds as he pulled off his jeans. Lastly there was something else, much lighter weight, that she could now hear being tossed aside.

Oh my God, he must be completely naked now. Her face reddened at this thought, but her telltale heartbeat raced.

She pulled her own blanket closer around herself and moved away.

"What are you doing?" he asked.

"Don't worry, don't worry," she blurted out quickly. "I'm not going to look at you." She tried to move farther away, but he pulled her back to face him.

"But I want you to look at me," he said softly.

She opened her mouth in surprise but could think of nothing to say. Her face burned again and she stared down at the floor to keep from meeting his eyes.

"Look at me," he said again, and he lifted her chin. Her eyes locked with his and she no longer felt embarrassed. Besides, she told herself, he was still mostly covered by the blanket.

Except that under the blanket he was naked.

She tried to forget about that as she settled deeper into her blanket and attempted to sleep.

Chapter 7

The Navajo Reservation

GINA WOKE UP sometime in the middle of the night. The fire had gone out. The air was cold in the little cabin, but she was warm along the line of her hip where Taro had nestled next to her.

The rain had stopped and moonlight now stretched across the floor. She glanced at Taro, tightly wrapped in his blanket, and watched his sleeping form rise and fall with his even breathing. *He looks so peaceful. And he is so beautiful.*

She carefully pulled away and sat up, trying not to disturb him.

Clutching her blanket, she went to the door and opened it, then stepped outside. A canopy of midnight blue, sprinkled with stars, stretched completely across the horizon. *A night wrapped in stars.* Mesas stood in shadow, like silent sentinels in the distance. She stood, transfixed by this scene, breathing in the crisp night air.

Suddenly she was not alone. Taro had awakened, and now joined her.

He gazed in awe at the beauty in the night sky, his eyes wandering across the horizon. It was like standing in a bowl full of stars.

"Millions and millions of stars," he said in a hushed voice.

They both looked up in appreciation. A full moon slid into view from behind a spire of rock, pale and silver.

"This is beautiful," he whispered.

"Yes it is."

"I have never seen the sky look like this before. So many stars, so much sky. And I have never seen the moon look so big. It makes me feel very small."

She smiled at him. "It's good to be reminded of that every once in a while. You can't experience this living in a city."

"No."

"I like to come up here when I can. It really clears my head."
"So, this is one of your special places?"
"Yes."
"I am glad you invited me to come here with you."
"Me, too."
They stayed out a little longer, until she said, "I'm getting cold. I'm going back inside."
He followed her in.
She pulled the sheets down on one of the beds and got in. He did the same with the other bed.

* * *

Gina woke up shivering, even though sunlight warmed her face. Suddenly she remembered where she was and bolted upright. Taro was sitting up on the other bed, looking over at her.
"Good morning," he said and yawned. "I was wondering when you would wake up."
"I was cold."
"Not me," he smirked. "I was nice and warm. You slept in your wet clothes all night."
A quick peek confirmed that he was still wrapped in his blankets.
"You look like a papoose," she teased.
"A what?"
"That's how some Indian women used to wrap up their babies. They rolled them into a blanket to stay warm."
"Well, it must have worked. I wasn't cold at all."
Gina glanced toward the fireplace where Taro's clothes still lay. A blush begin to burn across her face. She cleared her throat and turned to him. "I think I'm dry now. What do you say to getting out of here and finding some breakfast?"
"Sounds good to me," he answered cheerfully. "By the way, thank you again for inviting me up here. It's been fun. And last night, all those stars…"

While they waited for their breakfast, Gina sipped her coffee and gazed out the window to the parking lot, where Taro was making calls on his cell phone to the members of the band back in Phoenix. She watched him pacing back and forth talking and gesturing, and wondered what he was telling them.

He finished his conversation and ambled back into the restaurant. With a wide smile, he explained that the bus was now waiting for a part, so the band would be in Phoenix at least another day.

Thank God for broken-down tour buses! To him, she said, "We could spend another day up here, if you want. There's another special place I'd like to see. Do you want to go with me, or should I drive you back to Phoenix?"

"With you," he answered immediately. "Let's go!" And, after a few moments, "Where are we going?"

"Antelope Canyon."

"Antelope Canyon? What is that?"

"It's a slot canyon. It was formed from water carving through rock for millions of years. Very narrow walls with unusual light effects. I think you'll like it."

"Okay. Sounds good."

They made the drive north and west to Page.

The road was rough and twisted as they bumped along, bouncing in their seats. She was not bothered in the least by any of it, driving with the windows rolled down.

"I don't see any road signs, and we're in the middle of nowhere." He gestured across the landscape. "How do you know which way to go? Have you been here before?"

"No. Just look at the sun. It's in the east, so we go north and then west. There aren't many roads up here. We'll find it."

* * *

She talked as if this was the most natural thing in the world to do. Taro was impressed.

As she drove, he noticed how Gina seemed to feel completely at ease behind the wheel, sometimes waving at rock formations or other points of interest as they passed. She was wearing dark sunglasses, and the wind from the open window blew her hair in all directions, but she didn't seem to mind. She was not wearing makeup, he also noticed. Most of the women he had known would never want to be seen this way, with their hair all out of control and not even lipstick. It occurred to him that this girl was interested in a lot more than just looking good, although he did think she was pretty. She did not need to paint herself up to be interesting. He had to think about that, and decided he liked it.

* * *

They reached the town of Page about midday, where they made inquiries about the canyon. She drove to an area where they parked, purchased tickets and waited for a bus.

"Why can't we just go there by ourselves?" Taro complained.

"Because this is tribal land, and these are sacred sites. They only let tourists go into the canyon with an Indian guide. That way, they can keep people from damaging the walls of the canyon. It's the only way they can protect this land from people like us. Good for the Indians!"

He laughed, shaking his head, "You're funny."

"Maybe, but I don't blame these people for trying to preserve this land. It's all they have left, after our government took almost everything else. If I was a member of the tribe, I would do exactly the same thing."

Taro nodded, but she could see a hint of a smile.

After about twenty minutes, a bus arrived, rolling in with a cloud of dust and squealing brakes. Taro and Gina boarded along with other tourists. The next half-hour was spent in more bouncing around over dirt roads as the bus navigated the way to the canyon entrance.

"After this, your tour bus will probably feel like flying on a private jet," she teased.

He said nothing, but she could see a mischievous sparkle in his eyes.

When they arrived, the guide explained that the canyon walls were four hundred feet straight down, like deep narrow slits in the earth, leading into a hidden world beneath. They walked to the entrance, then made their way down into the canyon bottom.

Above them, fantastic plays of light and shadow curved around the steep sandstone walls in layers of color. An overall warmth in golden hues spilled downward, mixed with rays of sunlight streaming directly down onto the sandy floor. As the sun shifted overhead, the colors in the canyon walls also shifted, creating an atmosphere of unearthly beauty.

"This is unbelievable!" Taro whispered. "I have never seen anything like this. Like something in a dream."

After several hours walking through the canyon, they re-joined the rest of their group on the bus, bouncing in their seats all the way back to the parking area. They bought some burgers at a local fast-food place and wandered over the bridge spanning the Colorado River.

In the late afternoon, they drove back to the cabin, cleaned up before dinner, then walked back to the little local restaurant. Their waiter from the night before greeted them with a beaming smile.

"He seems happy to see us again," she remarked as they sat down.

Taro grinned. "I left him a nice tip last night."

"So did I. He seems like a nice kid."

They looked at each other and laughed.

After they ordered, Gina excused herself to go to the ladies' room. When she returned, she found Taro talking with their waiter.

"I saw him bring in a guitar and asked if he played. He has a band, and was interested to know I am also a musician. So we have been invited to a community dance for tonight. Miah's going to play with his band. What do you think?"

She smiled and nodded.

"Yes, we will be honored to come," Taro said to the waiter.

"This is so cool," Miah said, then he added, "We're only going to play a few songs. There'll be some other bands, too. It's kind of a community gathering. There's not much entertainment around here, so we make our own."

"I'm sure we will enjoy it," Taro said graciously.

After dinner, they strolled through the little town, past a school and some other buildings, and found the community center. The building was small and plain, but a large patio area extended out past an overhang in the back. Several bonfires were burning near groups of people sitting in fold-up chairs. As the crowd grew, Gina noticed that people of all ages were gathering here, together in one place.

Under the overhang, a band was already playing what sounded like a mix of country music and tribal melodies. Some people were dancing and others were listening. There was an atmosphere of unity everywhere.

The band finished their song, and another group joined them, bringing in a huge drum. They began singing a chant. Several young men joined the musicians, beating the drum. Some of the older spectators got up from their chairs and started circling around, keeping their steps in time to the drum. A few of them wore bells on their boots that added to the music.

When the song was over, another chant was started, and more people danced.

The chants finished. Miah and his group gathered in the stage area and started to play. They played rock and roll, but people danced to their music, too.

After several songs, Miah's group received loud applause from the crowd, especially the younger ones. Miah beckoned to Taro and Gina, and proudly introduced them to his friends. He also introduced them to his mother, a tall, lovely woman who thanked them for coming to hear her son play.

Miah and his band were eager to talk with Taro, asking his opinion on how they played. They discussed chords and other musical topics, while Gina talked with Miah's mother about turquoise jewelry and weaving.

A different group started to play, and everyone turned to listen. These musicians were older, and it was obvious they had been playing together a long time. The crowd moved closer. Gina listened, enchanted by what she heard. She noticed that Taro had stopped talking and was listening, too. The sweet sound of a native flute soared above Spanish style guitar work with native drums and other percussion. The vocals were different, too, with beautiful, distinctive harmonies.

Another song followed, this time more traditional.

Gina noticed that the dance area filled with women, dancing in a circle with precise steps.

"This is a woman's dance. Come, dance with us," Miah's mother invited her. She glanced at Taro, then said, "Will your man let you dance with us?"

Gina felt her face redden. She peeked over at Taro, who looked amused. He gestured with his head that she should join the dance, so she followed Miah's mother into the circle and tried to follow the steps. She was aware of a sense of some kind of ancient rhythm awakening within her as she moved, swaying and dancing in circular patterns with the other women.

* * *

Gina's hair gleamed gold and silver against the night, and as she swayed she almost looked like some kind of spirit, dancing freely on the breeze. Ethereal. Not of this earth; lifted above. Taro stood watching her, and found he could not look away.

How could he not think of her as beautiful, as he saw her now? Her face, warmed by light from the fires, the glow of her skin, the sparkling eyes, the soft smile, the inherent sensuality in her face and in her body motion as she moved; so essential, so primeval, part of the rhythm of all life. She was one with this world, he sensed, appreciating the idea. He watched her as she danced, some kind of earth-bound angel, like no one he had ever known before. He realized he was moving, too, moving toward her. As the song ended, and men started to join the women in the dance, she circled closer. Taro moved closer, too, and she floated into his arms.

They danced to this music, to words not known to either of them, but to rhythms awakening within. Surrounding them, the music rose around and above them, rising up the walls of the canyon, up to the stars. A sense of being in the flow of all life, in a deeply spiritual world not bound by time, infused them. What is, has always been, will always be, and they were now a part of that.

Warm light from the fires burnished their faces. In this light, her eyes shone with some kind of green fire that drew him to her. They gazed at each other in a way that they understood as a recognition of kindred souls, as if they had been moving toward each other since a time before time. They were warm together, eyes of green and darkest sable locking together.

They danced to almost every song after that.

At the end of the evening, they thanked Miah and his friends and family again for inviting them, and joined the others who were leaving for home.

Gina felt almost weightless on the walk back to the cabin. She looked up at the sky, where stars stretched as far as she could see.

Another night wrapped in stars, except that this time we're wrapped up in the stars, too. A wonderful, magical night.

Back in the cabin, they relaxed in front of the fire, talking and laughing, simply enjoying being with each other.

"Tonight made me remember when my band was just starting out," Taro confided. "We used to play for community groups like this. It was a chance for us to try out our stuff in front of an audience and get a reaction. We wrote a bunch of songs and recorded them ourselves and sold the CDs when we played.

"But we had a hard time trying to design a cover for the CDs. We decided to put a photo on the front, but couldn't agree on anything until I had the idea that we should all be standing under a "No Smoking" sign. With all of us smoking. Kind of a rebel thing." He raised his eyebrows and laughed. "Of course, the kids loved it, and we sold a lot of CDs.

She laughed too. "That was actually a good idea. Kids always like what they think their parents hate. So, I think you showed a lot of marketing smarts by doing that."

They grinned at each other.

It's like I have known him forever.

They snuggled together in the blankets, enjoying the colors in the fire and the closeness in the atmosphere of the little cabin, far away from the interference or demands of the outside world.

Several times, she woke up with a start, realizing that she must have fallen asleep next to him.

* * *

Sometimes Taro also drifted into sleep. When he awakened, the sense of peace in this place infused him with it, and he realized that he was happy.

He could just be, exactly as he was. He looked over at her. She met his eyes, and he was certain that she appreciated it, too, this sense of serenity.

No pressure, no problems, just tranquility, yet their senses had never felt so alive.

Somehow, together, they could just be.

Chapter 8

Phoenix

AT BREAKFAST THE NEXT MORNING, Taro called to confirm that the bus was repaired. "I need to be in Phoenix this afternoon," he explained. "The band will pick me up at your house on the way to Tucson for a show tonight. The day after that, we're scheduled for a show in Albuquerque."

"I guess we both have to go back to work now," she observed, buttering her toast. "This has been great, but when we get to Phoenix, it's back to the real world for both of us."

He sighed. "I guess so. But it would be nice if we could stay longer."

She smiled but also wondered if he wanted to stay because he liked the area, or being with her, or maybe both.

* * *

He helped her bring in her things from the Jeep, and they sat in the living room to wait. There was an awkward silence for a few moments. She turned on her radio to fill the space between them.

"The bus will be here soon. What do you want to talk about?" he asked.

Gina hesitated, suddenly unsure how to respond.

A slow, sultry song began to play. Impulsively, she rose to her feet. Holding her hands out to him, she said, "Come on—won't you dance with me?"

Taro blinked in surprise, but stood up and walked toward her. He took her hands in his, and they began to dance. He was somewhat formal at first, holding her at a distance, but then she looked up at him and smiled, and somehow they were closer.

He could feel her warmth and realized that he liked it. He could see that she liked it, too.

Sighing, he folded his arms around her, holding her against his body as they swayed to the music.

He's so warm, she thought, enjoying the nearness of him, wanting to stay in his arms forever.

When the song ended, they remained standing together, their arms around each other. Then she turned her face up to look at him, and their lips met.

Every old expression she had ever heard about fireworks going off seemed to be coming true as she moved closer, wanting his kisses, wanting to kiss him back, wanting everything.

He took her hand and led her to the sofa. They sat down and he pulled her into his arms, kissing her again, the lightest kisses, soft as feathers.

His nearness was intoxicating. She wrapped her hands in his hair and pulled his face closer. He kissed her again, now using just the tip of his tongue to touch all around the inside of her lips like little flicks of flame.

WOW. Just Wow. How did he learn to kiss like that? This was unlike anything she had ever felt before. So delicate, but so intense. Wow.

He leaned her back so that he was almost above her and kissed her again. This time she felt his tongue probing deeper into her mouth, and she could taste him.

Her breath caught in her throat when his hands moved down her body to stroke her.

"Oh, Gina, you are so soft," he whispered.

Suddenly, she hesitated.

What's wrong with me? Am I just shy? I'm finally with the man I've been dreaming about and he's driving me wild.

Realization hit her like a thunderclap. What if he didn't find her attractive enough or desirable enough? Would he think she was too fat, too anything, and reject her? For a moment she froze in panic and almost pushed him away. The thought of being rejected now, so close to what she wanted, unnerved her.

She heard him sigh, and her thoughts focused back to now and what he was doing to her.

"You feel so good," he breathed. He closed his eyes and kissed her through her clothes, then gently laid his cheek on her breast. "We don't have much time left," he said, and kissed her again.

Waves of sweet intensity swept over her and she relaxed, allowing the delicious sensations to wash over her completely. She reached up and caressed his cheek, thinking about how much she wanted him, how good it felt to have him here like this, his body on top of hers, and then she could feel something pressing against her so hard it hurt. She realized it was him, that he was aroused too, that the hardness was for her. And she wanted it. She wanted to tear off all their clothes and let him bury himself deep inside her.

Somebody started banging on the door. Shocked, they both bolted upright, staring at each other. Their eyes looked wild and their hair and clothes were disheveled.

The doorbell rang.

"It's the bus," he groaned, rolling his eyes and helping her up from the sofa. They only had a few seconds to straighten their hair and clothes before a series of loud honks sounded from outside. Through the front window they watched the rest of the band getting out of the bus, glancing around at everything, wary and cautious. She and Taro opened the door and waved for them to come in.

The tour bus was parked just beyond the sidewalk. Oh, great, she thought. Neighbors were staring and gawking, openly curious. To them, these guys must look like a group from another planet, with their wild-looking hair and black leather. The thought made her want to laugh.

Inside her house, there was joking and teasing. They all regarded her with extreme curiosity, but they were friendly and polite, smiling as they introduced themselves.

"We need to get going," one of them said after a few moments. The others agreed, moving back toward the door. "It was nice to meet you," they all said, on their way out.

Taro stood with her by the door. He took her hands in his. "Everyone needs to find someplace where it's quiet and you can think. Thank you for showing me your special place. Now, when I need to turn off the crazy stuff, I can come back here in my head." He leaned down and kissed her. "I have enjoyed being with you, but I must go now."

Speaking of coming back...

As though he could read her thoughts, he bent his head toward her until their foreheads touched. "I will call you. And I will come back to you again," he whispered. He turned and walked out to the bus. He stopped and waved to her just before walking up the steps. The door closed behind him, the engine revved up, and the bus pulled away.

The house seemed unusually quiet after they had all left. She tried to think about what she would need to do for work the next day, but it was almost impossible to concentrate on anything except Taro. It took her a long time to fall asleep.

* * *

The next morning she arrived for work the same time as Lynn.

"Good morning, Lynn," she chirped.

"You look happy today. You must have had a good time off," Lynn commented.

"Yeah, I did. It was great! I went up to the Rez and I got some wonderful new stones for my jewelry."

"Is that all?" Lynn drawled. "You seem extra excited or something."

"Do I?"

Lynn peered at her suspiciously. "You look excited and happy."

Gina smiled.

"A new man?"

"Well...yes. You just wouldn't believe it."

"Not Jason?"

"Absolutely not."

"What about Donny?"

"No."

"Who, then?" And after a moment, "Oh my God! Don't tell me!"

"Well, okay, yes, but nothing happened. He was very nice, so don't worry."

Lynn had stopped walking and stood staring.

"I'll probably never see him again, anyway, Lynn. He had to leave. We had dinner and then we went up to the Rez. And no, to answer your question, but it's not like I didn't think about it."

Lynn shook her head, laughing. "Oh, Gina, I just don't believe you went up there with someone like that—you don't even know him!"

"Trust me, Lynn, it's all good. He's really a nice guy. You'd like him if you knew him. Besides, I probably won't ever see him again, so please just chill, okay?"

"Okay, Gina, okay. I just can't believe you took off and rocked the Rez with someone you only met one time—and a musician, no less. I hope he was nice. I don't want to see you get hurt."

"I know," Gina sighed. "Thanks for your concern, but please don't worry."

"I thought Jason was nice," Lynn pressed. What happened there?"

"He's boring, Lynn. He just wants people to keep telling him how great he is because he had some winning touchdowns once upon a time. Not what I want to hear about for the rest of my life. I doubt if he's read any books since college, or had any original thoughts since God knows when."

"And Donny? I thought you were going to have dinner with him."

"No, he had to cancel—something about a meeting with a client. He's always going to be too busy. I don't want to be with a man who has to pencil me into his schedule. He's a hot-shot computer specialist. There will always be a crisis somewhere he has to fix, and his interests will always come first. I'd just have to live with it. That's how my family treated me. Why would I want more of that? I want to be important to someone; a man who can be more like a partner. Someone I can share everything with."

"Well, what about Barbara's cousin? He sounds really nice."

"I don't know, Lynn. Maybe he is," Gina sighed. "But honestly, I just don't have the time or energy to do the whole dating scene again. I don't want to wait around to see if someone grows on me. I don't want to play the getting to know you game."

Gina frowned. "I want a man who catches my interest right away. Someone who is smart and fun, and who doesn't just follow the same old path as everyone else. Someone who treats me well, who has good manners but isn't stuffy or tries to smother me with his ideas of how I should act or talk, or think. I've had enough of that to last a lifetime."

"Got it. I understand," Lynn said thoughtfully. "It sounds like the reason I left my first husband. He married me, expecting a cook and a maid, and everything had to be his way, or else. I'm a Texas rancher's daughter. I felt fenced in, so I left. Then I found Mike and we hit it off right away, so I do understand what you're saying. But I still think you should try to meet other people. You know, be willing to try something new. Take a chance with someone."

"Lynn, I just did. And I had a great time."

"Yeah, I can tell. What's his name again?"

"Taro."

"Okay. So you had a good time with Taro. But he's gone now. He's gone on with his life and so should you. Besides, what could you really have in common with someone like that?"

"What do you mean by 'someone like that', Lynn? Someone from another country? Someone in show business? You think he's some kind of wild and crazy rock star? You'd be surprised. I was surprised myself. We were together for two days and nights and he didn't try to push me into anything. I felt very comfortable with him…"

She stopped because Lynn was staring at her again.

"Lynn, he has all the qualities I want, but just because he's Japanese, it's not okay?"

"Well, no. That part doesn't bother me."

"Then, because he's a musician, it's not okay?"

"I don't know, Gina. Maybe. It just seems so different from your lifestyle. Y'all are such opposites from each other."

"They say that opposites attract," Gina argued.

Lynn relented. "Well, yes, sometimes they do."

Gina was quiet the rest of the way into the store, but in her head, conflicting ideas faced off.

Maybe she's right. Maybe I should be interested in meeting the friend, the cousin, or whoever else I can get introduced to…

But how can I do that when I know in my heart that I'm just not interested in any of them? How can I explain that my heart has already been taken by my heavy metal troubadour? How can I make Lynn see Taro as I do—a man with the soul of a poet, wrapped up in black leather?

Chapter 9

Early November—Phoenix/Sedona

DAMN! I'M GOING TO BE LATE!

After almost two months of phone calls and planning, what a time for the Weasel to show up in her office just before she left the store! He detained her for at least half an hour, discussing how he wanted some holiday fixtures set up. Gina fumed all the way to the airport.

She rushed to the baggage area and anxiously looked around. Through the crowd, she glimpsed Taro standing alone against a wall, wearing dark sunglasses. His hair fell past his shoulders, as black as the long leather coat he wore. He was not smiling, and didn't look like someone it would be easy to start a conversation with.

Gina called his name and rushed to him. She kissed his cheek and apologized for being late. He seemed relieved to see her, but did not return her embrace or smile.

"Let's go," he said. He picked up his suitcase and gestured for her to lead the way through the terminal.

Why is he so quiet? His silence bothered her. Gina's feeling of happiness wilted. Then she remembered what she had heard about how Japanese people detested public displays of affection. *Maybe I embarrassed him, greeting him like that, especially after I made him wait. Damn! Will I never learn?*

They reached her Jeep and she unlocked it. He threw in his bag and went around the other side to get in. Gina sighed. Maybe this hadn't been such a good idea after all. She had been so excited about seeing him, but maybe they should have left things as they were and never tried to meet again. As logical and sensible as that thought was, it brought her pain. She resented the intrusion of conflicting emotions within her.

Taro leaned back in his seat and took off the sunglasses. She noticed for the first time how tired he looked. Instantly, she softened in concern for him.

He turned to her and said quietly, "It is good to see you again." His intense dark eyes locked on her and his lips turned up in a trace of a smile. Gina's pulse jumped.

He is so beautiful.

Taro looked out the window most of the way, not saying much.

He sure seems moody. Or is he absorbed in some worry? In any case, she felt left out and wasn't sure if she should be concerned or irritated.

When they arrived at her house she parked and Taro pulled out his suitcase. Gina unlocked the front door and motioned him inside. *"Dozo,"* she said, and saw him smile.

He dropped his bag in the hall and closed the door as she went to get a hanger for his coat.

When she returned and reached for the coat, he stepped forward so that she touched him instead. She looked up, surprised. He bent down and kissed her, wrapping his coat around her as he held her against his chest. She sighed with relief and snuggled against him.

Taro kissed her again. She slipped her arms around him under his coat and moved into him. They stood locked together for a long time, then he took her hands in his and raised her arms, pressing her back against the wall with his body. He slowly moved his hands down her arms and over her body. His eyes closed and he sighed. Gina closed her eyes too, sure her knees were melting under her, but relaxed under the touch of his hands. She could feel his excitement swell as he pressed against her.

His caresses abruptly stopped. She opened her eyes to look up at him. He was smiling, his hands still warm on her body. "Tonight we have a lot of time," he whispered, stroking her with his fingertips. "Time just for us." He kissed her again and then released her from his embrace.

"But now, please, I would like to take a shower and change clothes from the trip."

What? I can't believe this! How can he shift gears so quickly?

In a daze, she managed to show him where the bathroom was and got out clean towels for him.

"Thank you," he whispered in her ear with a kiss. He stepped into the bathroom and closed the door.

She was left standing in the hall seething with a mix of confusion and growing anger. By the time she got back downstairs to the kitchen she was so furious she grabbed a spoon off the countertop and threw it across the room.

What the hell...? How dare he? How could he get me all excited like that and then leave me hanging with "Tonight we will have a lot of time"? He's got some nerve, coming into my house and setting me up like that. What the hell did he come back for, anyway?

Almost instantly, she realized he came back for the very same reason she wanted to see him again. Something magic had happened when they were together the first time. They both needed to know if it was the start of something more, or merely a nice one-time meeting that would make a pleasant memory.

"I think... no, I'm sure it was the start of something more. Much more," she reasoned aloud. *Oh, God, did I really say that? How corny can you get?*

At this, she laughed at herself, her anger gone. "But I'm sure he feels it, too," she stated, trying to convince herself that this was indeed the case. After all, didn't he hint of more delights to come for tonight?

But then, what am I hoping for? Sex? Oh, yes, that much at least. She was still excited from the touch of him moments ago, her panties damp from anticipation. But it was more than that. She wanted him there to talk to her, to tell her what he had been doing, his travels and impressions of the country, any new ideas he had for songs. She was hungry for the sound of his voice. She wanted to look at him—all of him. She wanted to know everything about him. Most of all, she wanted to know he enjoyed being with her, too.

She thought about the dinner she had planned for this evening. It would be perfect, she hoped. A wonderful, relaxing evening... and maybe much more.

The thought occurred to her that he might also have plans cooked up for tonight, and she wondered what that might entail. His behavior by the door hinted that he was interested in far more than just a visit to an old friend. Or was he checking her reaction to his advances? In any case, his mentioning time tonight 'just for them' had certainly gotten her attention!

"Well, two can play that game," she said to herself as an idea crept into her head. "I can flirt with you, too."

She listened. The shower upstairs was still running. She ran upstairs quickly and changed into a sexier outfit, rubbing her most erotic perfume into pulse points all over her body. She checked her hair and makeup and was satisfied, then returned to the kitchen and appeared to be extremely busy when he re-appeared.

He stood in the kitchen doorway, smiling, wearing a plain pair of jeans and a simple shirt. His hair was still wet from a shampoo. He looked refreshed, and she noticed that he had shaved.

"Here, won't you come and taste this?" she cooed, inviting him closer with her smile. "I'm not quite sure if this is sweet enough." She offered a spoonful of the chocolate pie she was making for dessert.

He fell for it. He stepped closer and she slipped the spoon into his mouth. When she withdrew the spoon, she leaned up against him and kissed him, waiting for his reaction.

His eyes closed, and as he reached for her, she backed him up against the counter. She took his face in her hands and kissed his nose, his eyes, his chin and down to his neck.

She heard his quick intake of breath but she abruptly stopped, kissed his cheek, and shooed him out of the kitchen.

He gave her a bewildered look, but then smiled at her knowingly, before walking into the living room. He sat down, watching her through the pass-through bar.

She opened a bottle of beer and walked out to hand it to him.

"I'm so glad you're here," she teased, and quickly retreated into the kitchen.

* * *

She could not see his broad smile and could not know how much he was intrigued with her little game. She had hinted at a promise of passion for the coming night, but he realized that she was showing him that she had her own mind, her own way of doing things, and her own sense of timing. He looked forward to what the night would bring, anticipating that her surrender to him would be sweet but would only happen when she was ready. He liked that. Something about her made him think that she would not waste her time with casual affairs, but when she was stirred to passion, her involvement was total.

Making her want him had to be quite an accomplishment, he thought, and tonight he planned to make her want him even more. He wondered what it would be like to totally ignite her passion, and felt warmed by the memory of her body pressing against him. He wanted more.

"I'm going to enjoy this," he said to himself. He relaxed and settled into his chair.

* * *

Back in the kitchen, Gina was a bit amazed at herself. *Dear God, what has come over me?* But she had to smile, too. He was so warm, so alive, so sexy. Being around him was driving her wild. She wanted to lay him out somewhere and kiss every inch of his beautiful body.

She thought back to how she had been raised to believe a woman should always act like a lady. She remembered how she had always felt obliged to feign shock, outrage, shyness, or some mixture of these when fending off the advances of the young men she knew then.

How things have changed. I've got this gorgeous man in my house, and he's a foreigner, no less, but I can hardly keep my hands off him. Her face burned with a blush.

Things were always so stiff and formal with most of the safe, clean-cut boys I knew, the kind my parents wanted me to marry, with good prospects for the future. The kind with such high opinions of themselves. The kind that never had time or understood me, or made me so nervous I couldn't be myself around them. Now here is a man the complete opposite of everything I've been around all my life. Someone who will never look like the nice young boy next door, who will grow up to belong to the country club and be a bank vice-president or something. Here's someone who is a real free spirit, a musician with long hair, and Japanese to boot. It's a totally impossible situation, yet I'm fascinated with him. He's smart and nice and totally hot. I could lick him from his ears all the way down to his toes. I would have never imagined something like that with the other guys I've known. Trying to act like a lady always got in the way, and I let it because it seemed so important.

But, she warned herself, sometimes if you didn't reach out for what you wanted, the chance was gone forever. Taro was definitely worth reaching out and grabbing.

She did not want to miss this chance to be with him, to touch him, and hopefully make love to him. They were such an impossible mix that it would be ridiculous to think of a future. Any future with this man was out of the question—there simply was none. All they had was this short time now. She could not, would not, risk letting this chance go by. This was what she wanted, and she knew with certainty that she would not change her mind. Memories of his eyes had haunted her day and night. She knew she had wanted him from the start and could not get him out of her mind. She had to take the chance.

* * *

They sat on the floor together while they ate dinner, leaning back on oversized stuffed pillows that served as chairs. She had draped the coffee table with lengths of cloth, and placed everything within easy reach. The mood was warm and casual. She made several batches of drinks with a blender, and then they took turns making more.

Strange shapes appeared and flickered across the walls from a group of candles, now the only illumination in the room.

In this light, Taro's eyes sparkled. His skin had never looked so smooth, she thought. *Like polished alabaster.* His hair, now dry, tumbled down past his shoulders like lengths of black satin. There was a warmth in his face that came more from contentment than the drinks. This realization alone made all her dinner preparations worthwhile.

For a time after they finished eating, they sat quietly together, saying nothing, simply enjoying this time together.

When she rose to clear the dishes, he reached for her hand and said, "Leave them. Stay here with me." His hand closed around hers and he pulled her back down to the floor.

He held her loosely in his arms, looking into her eyes, and leaned forward to kiss her. She knew she was trapped but had no wish to be free. She kept her eyes open until his face filled all the space she could see, then she closed her eyes as the warmth of his lips pressed against hers. Their noses bumped, and he laughed, kissing her nose.

They leaned together again for another kiss, then he gently pulled her against his side and rolled over next to her so they were lying on the floor face to face.

He reached for her again and she moved closer. He teased her mouth with his tongue, kissing her with little licks just inside her lips. *Like little flicks of fire.* She wrapped her hands in his hair, pulling his face to her. Her tongue caressed his, then moved deeper into his mouth, enjoying the taste of him. He responded at once with deeper kisses of his own, his hands moving down her body to caress her. He cupped her breasts in his hands, enjoying her soft fullness, a promise of sweetness yet to come. He kissed her breasts through the fabric of her dress, then slowly moved her onto her back and carefully positioned himself over her, nuzzling her face with more kisses.

The nearness of him was intoxicating. She felt his weight settle down over her body and could feel his erection pressing against her. *He is so hard. So hard. And I want him.*

"You feel so good," she breathed.

"So do you," he said, his breath ragged.

"Where is your bedroom?" he asked hoarsely, trying to concentrate on the words. He knew he must try to cool down to keep from losing control because all his senses screamed for him to take her now.

"Upstairs. Come on," she whispered

She picked up one of the candles that was still burning. Hand in hand, they made their way upstairs in the flickering darkness. She led the way into her room and set the candle down on her dresser, then walked over to the bed and pulled back the covers.

She slid across the sheets, and he followed her.

They clutched eagerly for each other in the semi-darkness.

Taro's hands caressed her. Gina shivered with intense pleasure and met his eyes. She could see desire there, but also hesitation, as if he was waiting for some kind of sign from her.

"You are so beautiful," she whispered truthfully, touching his cheek. "You are the most beautiful man I have ever seen."

He blinked in surprise. In one motion, he propped himself up on one arm and pulled her to him. The buttons on her dress gave way, then it was gone. He pulled open her bra, and it was gone, too, then he was all hands and mouth, loving her. His fingers stroked her bare skin, then the wet warmth of his mouth pulled in the soft flesh of her breast, sucking gently and caressing her nipple with his tongue.

"So sweet," he whispered. "So sweet." He cupped her breasts in his hands and licked across the tips.

She could feel herself filling with the molten fire of desire. An aching was growing inside her that was almost painful. She began to thrash around under him.

He reached for her hand and brought it to the front of his jeans, holding it against him as he brought the zipper down. She could feel his heat, and needed no urging to reach inside his jeans to stroke him with her fingertips. His breath caught in his throat. He scrambled furiously to free himself from his clothes, and he came to her again, bringing her hands back to caress him.

Her heart beat faster in excitement. *He is so hard and so warm*. She rose to her knees next to him and stroked him, loving his perfect shape, the warm rounded tip, the hard, straight shaft. She bent closer so she could take him into her mouth, licking across the tip, tasting him, then down his length and back again. She heard him groan in pleasure.

He was so aroused that even his teeth ached. He knew he couldn't wait much longer, but he wanted this union to be perfect for her; and for that to happen, he wanted to be sure she was ready. She must want him so much that there would be no turning back. He wanted to take her past the point for any shyness, games or pretense, past the barriers to where wanting became need.

His hands moved over her body again, stroking her inner thighs, then the space between her legs, finding her warm sticky wetness. He smiled, knowing the wetness was for him. His fingers reached deep inside, opening her. She began to quiver uncontrollably as he reached inside her again and again until she wanted to scream her need for him.

"Do you want me?" he breathed into her ear.

"Yes," she whispered back.

Tenderness and desire glowed in his face. He lowered his eyes shyly, but then glanced up again, boldly meeting her gaze, with an expression of undisputable longing. A searing heat pulsed through her body, scorching her. He whispered, "Do I need condom?" and held out his hand with a silver packet.

"No." She closed his hand over the packet. Her face burned as she said the words but she gazed directly into his eyes. "I'm on the pill. I want to feel you, not plastic."

As her words registered, his eyes seemed to widen. A slow smile crept across his face.

"*Soka*. Then, put me in," he said, so quietly she almost couldn't hear him. She looked up into his eyes, and they were huge, gazing into hers, dark with passion. She could feel the heat of his desire, knowing it matched her own. "Put me in," he whispered again. "Put me in you."

She took him tenderly into both her hands and positioned him to the source of her wetness and opened herself to him. He pushed against her opening gently, then she could feel the shape of him entering her. She gasped with pleasure at the sensation of his warmth. He moved slowly at first, pushing a little farther in with each thrust. She was so slippery that it was easy for him to slide all the way into her. His warmth filled her and she almost wept in her joy. *He feels so good, even better than I could have imagined.* She moved with him, meeting his thrusts with motion of her own, in a rhythm as old as time.

She faded into weightlessness, lifted out of her own body as she floated up into a soft blue consciousness. It was like floating in a calm, misty sea where soothing blue-green water merged into a soft, silky fog, into the comforting world of the senses. Always before, she had kept herself from drifting away completely. She had still been moored to the dock of her fears, always wondering how she must be appearing to her partner. Always, there had been the fear of being judged on appearance and performance, and so always she had been essentially alone.

But this time she was not alone. They blended together, moving as one, cutting all ties with the familiar, the old land of insecurities and fears, like a ship sailing out to sea, free at last. He was her partner, he was her destination. They floated together in their newfound union, out into an uncharted, warm consciousness on waves of absolute tranquility and intense pleasure. The waves grew higher as they floated on and on, until at last the waves broke inside her and they became like two pieces of driftwood tangled up together, thrown together onto a new shore.

"He's a cuddler," she thought dreamily as a sense of the present slowly filtered back into focus. How long had they been lying together like this, she wondered. Had he still been inside her when they drifted into sleep?

Even now, he lay sprawled on top of her, his cheek resting on her breast, his arms wrapped around her. She could feel his soft, even breathing, so she knew he was sleeping peacefully. That was all she wanted to know at the moment, and she smiled as she floated back into dreamy oblivion, joining him in sleep.

Twice later, sometime during the soft blackness of the night, he awakened her with more kisses and caresses, and his ardent hardness filled her again and again. Together, they shared the rise of passion, the filling, the emptying out and refilling again as they experienced their coming together into completeness, a new union from what had been two separates.

Chapter 10

IN THE MORNING, Gina awakened first. Wanting to let him sleep, she tiptoed from the bedroom for a shower, then headed downstairs for coffee.

She thought about making breakfast for him, liking the idea. Moving around in the kitchen, her unaccustomed soreness made her smile, just remembering.

"Wow! What a night!" she voiced out loud, leaning back against the refrigerator, hugging herself and blushing. It was hard to believe everything that had happened, but it was real. It really was. Her soreness alone was proof of that. But, even more than that, an inner glow radiated out from her in all directions. At that moment she loved the whole world.

She scooped up Cheddar and nuzzled her ears. Cheddar exhibited a smile, closed her eyes halfway and purred, even after being set back down.

After a cup of coffee, Gina returned upstairs.

Soft light filled the room, illuminating Taro sleeping, his black hair spilled over the pillow. As though in an attempt to keep warm, he had burrowed under the bedcovers, but one bare shoulder and part of his arm were visible. Remembering the silky warmth of his skin, intense longing for him stirred within her.

She sat on the edge of the bed and stroked his hair.

A slight movement rippled under the covers, and he sighed, the sound like a purring deep in his throat. He moved closer, snuggling against her body, a soft smile on his lips.

Overwhelming feelings of tenderness and passion flooded through her. She bent to kiss his cheek, his eyes, his nose, his lips. He sighed again, beginning to awaken. His eyes opened and focused on her, his face still drowsy from sleep.

"Good morning," she whispered.

He reached for her, pulling her close. "Good morning," he replied, gazing at her with his beautiful sleepy eyes, yawning. He smiled. "Are you happy?"

"Yes."

"Yes," he echoed. "Happy." His smile was radiant.

"Are you hungry? I'm making you breakfast."

His eyes widened in surprise. "Really?"

"It's almost ready. I'll be right back." She jumped up to run downstairs to the kitchen and returned, bringing a tray.

He glanced at the tray, then back at her, grinning. "Thank you."

He sat up and she set the tray down beside him. She gave him a warm, moist washcloth so he could freshen his face and hands before eating. Plates were quickly uncovered, and he watched as she poured hot syrup over the pieces of toast.

"This is good, *ne?*" he said, nodding his approval after his first forkful. "What is it?"

"French toast. I hope you like it… what does 'ne' mean?"

"Isn't it? It's like an agreement to whatever was just said."

She smiled. "It sounds cool *ne?*"

He was hungry, pouring on extra syrup and eating it all.

Watching him, she thought again of the night before and snickered to herself. *He certainly has a healthy appetite! I'd like to pour that syrup all over his body and lick it all off.*

After they finished eating, he set the tray on the floor. "Come back into bed with me," he urged. He pulled back the covers, and she snuggled in next to him. He yawned and smiled. "Stay with me." His arms wrapped around her.

Taro unbuttoned the front of her gown, slipping his hands inside the fabric to touch her skin and turned her onto her side. "Sleep now," he whispered, nestling against her back, kissing the nape of her neck.

As she drifted into sleep, the last thing she remembered was feeling cherished, wrapped in his arms. Nothing else in the world mattered to her now. They were together and there was nowhere else she wanted to be.

They slept for several hours, until it was time for her to get ready for work. "I have to close the store tonight," she explained, "so I'll be back late. I left some food in the refrigerator for dinner. You can heat it up when you want. I'll take a sandwich with me to the store."

"We can go out for a late dinner, if you want," he offered.

"Maybe another time. I have to get up extra early tomorrow for a meeting."

"Okay. I'll get something to eat here and wait for you to get back."

She smiled. "Then, I'll see you later," she said, bending down to kiss his cheek.

"*Jaa, mata,*" he called as she walked through the doorway.

She turned back to him with a questioning look.

"*Jaa, mata.* It means I'll see you again later."

* * *

When she returned home, Taro was at the door to greet her, wrapping his arms around her and pulling her inside.

"I have surprise for you." He disappeared into the kitchen and returned with a chilled glass of wine for her.

"Thanks. This is great." She sipped the wine, enjoying the cold, sweet flavor.

"Here's to our second night together." He bent to kiss her, his hands reaching for the zipper in the back of her dress.

She pulled back to gaze into his eyes. His face wore the same look of longing as the night before. The thought sent a thrill through her.

"I think we should go upstairs now," he whispered.

She nodded. He took her hand and they walked upstairs to her bedroom.

He lit a candle and turned back to her, pulling the zipper on her dress completely down and easing it from her shoulders. She heard the soft sound it made as it fell to the floor. She stepped out of the dress and kicked it aside. Taro slowly removed everything else she was wearing, gazing at her in appreciation before he undressed himself. Enfolding her in his arms, he rolled with her to the center of the bed and caressed her body with kisses. He moved underneath her and pulled her over and on top of him, opening her legs and pushing up into her.

She gasped and leaned down to kiss him.

Gently, he pushed her back upright. "I want to look at you. All of you. You have a beautiful body and I want to look at you while I'm inside you," he whispered.

"And I want to look at you, too," she said. "All of you."

Saying that to him seems so natural. I've never said that to a man before.

Much later, she lay awake, gazing over at him. The candle was still lit, filling the room with a soft golden haze. Taro was awake, too, lying on his back looking at her. His eyes sparkled and he was smiling.

He had the most beautiful body she had ever seen—well-developed shoulders and arms, long, slim legs, flat stomach, and beautiful silky skin that was always warm. She liked it that he had no hair on his chest; she loved touching his smooth skin. Hair would just get in the way.

Compared to the almost delicate smoothness of his skin, when she thought back to most of the other men she had known, she saw them as excessively hairy, excessively fleshy, often overweight, lump-like; and the thought of making love to one of them repulsed her.

She rolled over, kissing all the way down his body until she reached to where he did have hair, finding his pink hardness waiting for her touch. She reached for it with her tongue and it responded by moving toward her.

She thought about jokes she had occasionally heard about Asian men lacking the size of other men. *That's hard to believe.*

Taro was built just fine, she thought. Nothing lacking there. He was regular size, about the same as all the others she had seen. But what he could do to her; how he made her feel. How perfectly he fit into her, how warm he was, and how good he felt inside her. She was glad she was on the pill. She wanted nothing to diminish the feeling of him inside her when they made love; no barriers between them.

* * *

"I'm going to kill that alarm clock!" Gina sputtered. She glanced at Taro, who was awake now, too.

He yawned, gazing at her with one eye shut. "Don't you have that planning meeting this morning?"

"Yes, and I need to hurry or I'll be late."

She vaulted out of bed and ran into the bathroom for a quick shower.

"I'll be back this afternoon," she told him when she returned to the room and got dressed. And tomorrow is my day off. I want us to go up to Sedona."

He raised his eyebrows at this, so she explained. "There's a shop up there that's interested in carrying some of my jewelry, so I have a meeting with the store owner tomorrow. Besides, I think you'll enjoy the area."

"I'll go with you anywhere," he declared. "So far, you have taken me to places I never knew about until I met you. But tonight, I'm taking you to dinner somewhere."

"Sounds good to me," she whispered, leaning into him with a kiss. "See you later."

Gina arrived a few minutes late, but no one noticed. Everyone was moving around and socializing before the meeting started. She picked up a cup of coffee and a glass of water and found a seat next to Lynn.

"Well, stranger," Lynn drawled. "I haven't had a chance to catch up with you lately, but I guess we've both been busy."

"Yeah," Gina agreed.

"Hey, I'm off tomorrow, too," Lynn continued. "Are you still planning to drive up to Sedona? I can go with you if you want."

"I've already got plans to go with someone else, but thanks for the offer."

"Really? With who?"

"Oh, I've got company here this week," Gina explained, waving her hand dismissively. "I guess I forgot to mention it. We're planning to drive up tomorrow morning."

"Oh," Lynn said. "Well, maybe next time."

"Yeah, sure," Gina mumbled, trying to stifle a yawn.

Lynn was instantly alert.

"What's the deal with you? Didn't you get enough sleep last night?'

"No, not much," Gina said, and immediately blushed scarlet.

Lynn's head jerked up. "Okay, so who's the company? You must have been up all night."

"Shhh," Gina whispered. "Don't talk so loud."

"Sounds like a man's involved. Someone new?"

"Well, not really," Gina admitted, lowering her eyes.

Lynn leaned closer. "Who?"

Gina blushed again.

Lynn narrowed her eyes and stared, and Gina imagined she could see the thoughts tumbling in her mind. Lynn made a kind of snorting noise. "Not…?" she asked, making a gesture to indicate long hair.

Gina nodded, staring down at the table.

"Oh, my God!" Lynn exclaimed. "He's here? The Japanese guy?"

"Yes," Gina confirmed in a whisper. "I didn't want to tell you yet. I wasn't sure how things would go."

"Well," Lynn announced with certainty, 'Things' must be going well. That would explain that goofy, dreamy look you had all day yesterday. I should have known. Are you sure you know what you're doing?"

"I think so," Gina said and blushed again. "Please, Lynn, just keep this to yourself. I don't know how this will work out, but so far it's been wonderful."

"I can see that," Lynn retorted. "Don't worry. I won't say a word to anybody, not even Mike. Just please, be careful."

"I will."

After that exchange, it was hard for Gina to pay attention to what any of the buyers said. She realized she really wasn't interested in hearing about floor plans or any of the new fashion trends being discussed. All she could think about was the vision of Taro, lying naked in her bed, his eyes sparkling in the candlelight.

Chapter 11

Sedona

They rose early in the morning and took a shower together.

My God, just when I thought maybe I was dreaming about how beautiful he is, I can see it's not my imagination. Not at all. He is absolutely real. Dear Lord help me, I want him so much.

They took turns washing each other's hair and bundled up in towels when they stepped out of the shower. While he shaved, he watched in fascination as she squeezed hair gel onto her hands and into her hair, and then combed her hair out straight.

"What?" she asked. "Don't you have to do something like that to your hair, too?"

"No, it just grows out straight." He picked up a strand of her hair and sniffed it. "Your hair smells like vanilla and honey. I like it."

Over the noise of two hair dryers running at once, Taro asked, "This place we're going—what's so special about it? You didn't really explain."

"Well, Sedona is kind of a quirky little town…"

"What's quirky?"

"Kind of offbeat, a little different, unique. The scenery is spectacular. Huge red rocks. A bit of the old West, but it's also a resort area. There are a lot of interesting shops and art galleries; that kind of thing. It's hard to describe, but you'll see when we get there."

"Okay." He laughed and pointed to the reflection of the two of them in the mirror, both holding hair dryers.

When they returned to the bedroom to get dressed, Gina suggested, "You might want to pack a change of clothes, just in case we decide to stay longer."

"Good idea." He reached for a small overnight bag and pulled out some clothes from his suitcase, then went back to the bathroom and returned with his shaving kit and toothbrush. He folded the clothes and put everything into the bag.

Gina pulled a suit from her closet and zipped it into a garment bag. She placed it next to her overnight bag on the side of the bed.

Taro raised his eyebrows at the suit, so she explained, "I need to put this on before I meet with the store owner. I can change clothes at a gas station right on the edge of town."

She scanned the room to make sure she had packed everything. "Oh! I almost forgot the shoes." She pulled a pair of black heels out of the closet and stuffed them into the bag.

Taro watched her, an amused smile on his face. "Are you sure you have everything now?"

"Yeah, now I do. My samples are downstairs, all packed and ready to go." She turned to look at him. "Men have a much easier time getting dressed," she complained. "All you really need is a shirt and a pair of pants."

"That's not really true. Men get dressed up, too. Sometimes I've had to wear a suit. With a tie."

She snickered. "Well, I bet you looked good. I bet you'd look good in a tuxedo, if you had to." *Taro in a tux. Wow, there's a picture I'd like to see.*

* * *

They drove north on Interstate 17.

Taro was quiet for a long time, staring out the window, but after a while he turned to her, shaking his head and laughing. "I love the names you have for places out here in the west. Like something out of a Road Runner cartoon. Names like Rock Springs and Sunset Point, but my favorite is Horse Thief Basin. What a name! But it was on a highway sign, so I know it's real. Unbelievable!"

Gina laughed. "Yeah, that's the wild west for you. Back in those days, it was a serious crime to steal a horse. They used to hang people for that."

"Really?"

"Oh, yeah. Back then, if you took someone's horse and left them stranded out here in the desert, they could die. It was considered one of the worst things anybody could do. Except for killing people, that is."

He laughed. "I still think it's a funny name."

When they reached the exit for Sedona, Taro leaned forward in anticipation. "I don't see any red rocks. Didn't you say this place is famous for that?"

"Just wait. You'll see."

He leaned back in his seat.

After driving for about another half-hour, Taro suddenly straightened up and pointed. "Look! I can see red in the mountains!"

"And this is only the beginning. I think you'll like it here. It's like no place else." She looked over at him before she continued. "I love Arizona. The real Arizona, like up here."

Taro nodded as he scanned the views on both sides of the road. He pointed to a massive rock formation. "It really is red."

Gina smiled. "There are a lot of others like that up here. One of them is called Coffee Pot because of its shape."

They rounded a curve, and ahead they could see a kind of valley, bordered on both sides by giant red rocks that stretched into the distance.

Taro whistled. "This looks like western movies I saw as a child. Has this place always been like this?"

"Yeah, except now the resorts have moved in, so these rocks are some of the most expensive in the world. There are a lot of interesting shops that sell really beautiful, unique things. All at very high prices."

They were lucky enough to find a parking place close to Old West Emporium, and strolled through the wide entryway. Greeting them were attractive displays of western wear, pottery, jewelry, t-shirts, and other western-themed items, including stacks of beautiful Navajo rugs. The air was filled with a pleasant leather smell, mixed with sage and vanilla from the candles and displays of scented soaps. Everything was clean and neatly arranged. Aisles led off in several directions, inviting people to slow down and browse through all the store offered.

"They have a lot of really cool stuff in here," Taro commented. I'll look around while you have your meeting."

"I'm a little nervous, Gina confessed. "I hope the lady I'm going to see will like my jewelry enough to order some of it. Her aunt is one of my customers over in Scottsdale, and she set up this meeting."

She went to meet the store owner.

* * *

"Taro! She likes it! She just placed an order. Isn't that great?"

"Yes, it is. Now you're really a successful jewelry designer. I think you can sell a lot in this store." He beamed with enthusiasm.

Gina glowed. "All I have to do is change the wording on the signs and tags to say 'Hearts of Sedona' instead of 'Hearts of the Earth'. That's easy to do. I'll be back up here in two weeks with my first order."

He grinned.

"This calls for a celebration!" she announced. "There's a place up here that's famous for its ice cream. All natural and home made. I'm going to buy you the biggest ice cream cone you ever had."

His eyes sparkled. "That sounds good. Chocolate is my favorite."

They ambled down the sidewalk to the ice cream shop, and came out with triple-scoop cones.

"*Oishii.* You're right. I think this is the best ice cream I ever had."

She raised her eyebrows. "What is *oishii?*"

"Delicious." He smiled.

They sat on a bench to enjoy their cones. Slanted rays of afternoon sunshine warmed them. It was a perfect early fall day.

"Your hair is so light," he observed. "I like it." He picked up a strand. "It looks almost white in this light."

"Well, I am descended from Vikings, you know," she teased. "From long ago."

"Really? They were fierce warriors, weren't they?"

She nodded. "Well, what about you? Are you from an old Samurai family?"

"Yes, but that was a long time ago."

"So, they were warriors, too, *ne*?"

"The Viking and the Samurai," he said, shaking his head and laughing.

"They were from two different parts of the world. I wonder what would have happened if they ever had met," she said playfully.

He was grinning now. "Maybe a war. Or at least a fight."

"Hmmm," she mused. " I wonder. Who would have won?"

"I don't know. Probably the Samurai."

"Oh, really?"

"Yes… maybe." He leaned closer to whisper in her ear. "But if they were anything like us, they wouldn't get much fighting done."

"True."

They spent the afternoon browsing through the shops, ending up back in the Old West Emporium.

"Hey, look at this!" Taro called to her. "What do ya think, little lady?" he said in his best imitation of a John Wayne voice.

Gina turned to see Taro wearing a black cowboy hat and had to laugh.

"What? Haven't you ever seen an Asian cowboy before?"

"Maybe in a Jackie Chan movie."

He grinned at her. "This is so cool. I'm going to get this for Chazz. He's always wanted one of these."

"Actually, it looks good on you," Gina said.

"Really? Maybe I should get one, too, but I was thinking about some cowboy boots. I always wanted some when I was a kid."

Gina laughed. "Well, let's see what they have."

They looked through the selection of boots in the store. He decided to try a black pair with a western design tooled into the leather.

"What do you think?" he asked her.

"They're really nice, but expensive. Why don't we look in some of the other stores?"

"No, I like these and they fit. Besides, since you will be selling your jewelry here, I feel good that I am buying something from here," he declared, a look of satisfaction on his face.

* * *

For dinner, they picked a restaurant featuring a patio that jutted out over the creek, so they could hear water flowing along the rocks in Oak Creek Canyon as they ate.

"Let's walk," she suggested after dinner, pointing up into the hills. "There are some million dollar homes up here. With views that are out of this world."

"Okay," he agreed. He reached for her hand as they walked.

"You know, it is unusual in Japan to see people walking together like this," he chuckled.

"You mean, holding hands?"

"Yeah. Most Japanese people do not show affection in public, like holding hands and kissing."

"Why not?"

"I don't know. It's just the way it is. But in America, people have different ideas. It seems very natural here."

"Yeah, I guess so. Couples here walk like this all the time."

"At first it was a little hard to get used to."

"So, why are we doing it, then?"

He tried to explain. "Well, we are in America, not Japan. And no one is out here except us, so there is nobody to see."

"Oh." She wasn't sure how she felt about this.

"But I kind of like it." He stopped and smiled at her.

"Oh, okay." She stopped walking and looked up at him.

He held her hand firmly in his and started back down the path. She moved with him.

Their breaths came in puffs from the chilly night air as they walked. Gina made a mental note to remind herself how warm his hand felt around hers.

The moon was full overhead, a circle of gold, hazing everything around them in a shimmery, dreamlike glow. A few houses were visible in the distance, but no one else was out, and the night was very quiet.

"Taro, why did you name your band Moonstorm?"

He was quiet for a few moments before he replied. "In Japan, we have festivals for all kinds of things. In fall we have festivals for moon viewing. In the old days, when most Japanese lived in the country, families got together to celebrate. People wrote poems and had special food. Some people believed if the moon was clear, it was a good omen for the next year. If the moon was covered by clouds, it was not a good sign."

"It sounds a lot like the ideas about the Harvest Moon we have here," she said. "But you don't hear much about it anymore, at least not in the cities."

"I think it is the same in Japan," he agreed. "Out in the country you would hear more about the old traditions than you would in the cities."

"That's a shame," she said thoughtfully. "I think there is a lot of beauty in some of the old traditions, and they're being lost now."

He nodded. "When I was a child, my family went to moon viewing festivals with my grandparents. It was always a special time. I remember thinking how beautiful the moon looked, so perfect and peaceful.

"Later, in school, we studied maps of the moon. I was shocked to see all the craters and mountains. The teacher told us that the surface looked that way because of volcanoes and meteor storms." He laughed. "I loved the idea of meteor storms and tried to imagine how they would look. I thought of storms with thunder and lightning like we have on earth, but with parts of meteorites raining down. Like something in science fiction."

He had stopped talking. Gina smiled at him, encouraging him to continue.

"When I got seriously interested in music I realized that I should keep the appearance of being what my parents and teachers expected, but inside, I was starting to think differently. In Japan, it is difficult to be an individual. People are taught very early to conform. We have a saying, 'The nail that sticks out will be hammered down'. I did not want to be that nail."

So, why were you so different?"

"I had a lot of new ideas but I did not want to talk about them with anyone yet. I knew I must keep a calm appearance, like the moon. I did not want to use up my energy in useless fights with my parents and school, so I was free to work on something new and different. Something I wanted."

Frowning in concentration, she offered, "I think that kind of conflict must happen with all truly creative people. There's always a choice to make. Either you see and do everything just the same as everybody else, or you see something different. Then you can create something new. That's much harder. But, just imagine, if nobody ever had a different idea, there would be no art or music or poetry in the world. It would be a boring world where everyone would be exactly the same."

The expression on his face was pensive. "I agree. And I think you are very much like this, too," he said softly. "On the surface you can be calm, but under that I can tell that you have strong ideas of your own. My experience with most Americans is that they say whatever is the latest popular expression—like 'awesome' about everything. You know what I mean. Sometimes it's hard for me to know if I can believe what people say here. Maybe they repeat what they hear on television so they don't really have to think."

He stopped walking and pulled her close. "But you—you say what is on your mind, and I think you really mean what you say. And you are creative. You have your own opinions, but you do not like to argue with people. So, you are like Moonstorn too," he smiled and touched her cheek. "My American Moonstorm."

She sucked in her breath quickly at this. *Did he say 'my'? My, as in, belonging to him?*

They walked in silence for a time and stopped to admire moonlight dancing on the water of a small creek. The sparkling water made the only sounds in the quiet night. Taro put his arms around her, pulled her closer, and kissed her. His lips were cold at first from the night air, but his tongue was very warm in her mouth. She moved closer into his embrace, wanting his nearness.

"Taro," she whispered, after several minutes of his delicious kisses, "You know what you just said about me saying what I really think?"

"Hmmm?,"

"What if I told you I want to make love to you right now?"

"Now? Here?"

"Yes. Here. Now," She leaned into him.

He stared at her, liking the idea. Her softness against his body was already making him aroused, and he thought back to the nights they had already spent together. He smiled. "Where?"

"Let's find a place," she said breathlessly. "A quiet, private place where we can be all alone and no one can see us."

"Maybe over in those trees," he suggested, now committed to the idea.

Hand in hand, they ventured into the woods, too far in to be seen by anyone, and found a space between some trees. After checking carefully to be sure no one was around, they put their jackets on the ground and lay down together. It was quite dark in the little hollow, as the thick branches over them obstructed most of the moonlight.

As he started to unbutton his shirt, his heart was racing. He couldn't believe she had suggested this. Just thinking of the possibility aroused him even more.

The night air was colder than he expected. "Are you really sure you want to do this? It's cold out here!"

"I don't care if there's snow on the ground!" she hissed. "I want you."

He expelled a long breath of air and reached for her. They fumbled with their clothes and soon they were naked together. With kisses and caresses they hungrily explored each other. At last, feeling how slickly wet she had become, he could wait no longer and pushed into her. They began their dance of love, where he, above her, moved in and out of her, meeting her upward motions in perfect rhythm.

Aurora Dawning

The heat they created together made them forget the cold night air.

She clung to him, never wanting to let him go. Each time she felt him thrust into her, she felt she would lose control completely and float over the edge, but she wanted him with her for that.

Just when the sweet intensity was almost suffocating, she heard him cry out her name as he exploded inside her, and they tumbled together into their world of bliss.

They cuddled together, panting, in the nest of their clothes. She could not imagine how long they lay there together, nor did she care. All that was important was that he was with her.

In the darkness, she could see the shine of his teeth as he smiled. "I was right about you," he whispered to her. "You are my American Moonstorm."

She smiled, snuggling closer.

"Let's stay here tonight and go back to Phoenix in the morning," he suggested. When do you have to be back at the store?"

"Not until tomorrow afternoon."

He grinned. "Good, then it's settled. I'm sure we can get a hotel room here."

"Well, if we're going to check into a hotel, we'd better get our clothes back on and straighten ourselves up a bit, don't you think?" she teased.

"Yeah," he grinned, reaching for his pants.

* * *

In a hotel advertising rooms overlooking the creek, they entered a spacious lobby decorated completely with western-style furniture. A gigantic stone fireplace warmed the room, setting off the oversized sofas and Navajo rugs on the floor.

Taro inquired about a room for the night. The desk clerk apologized that they were completely booked, "except for the Honeymoon Suite."

Gina was just about to say that it would probably be too expensive and that they should look elsewhere when she heard Taro say, "We'll take it."

He pulled out a credit card and gave it to the clerk, who responded with "Very good, sir. Just a moment." He punched some keys on a computer and moved to the counter behind him to print out the receipt.

In short order, the clerk returned the receipt and credit card, handed the room key to Taro, and mentioned something about a complementary bottle of champagne. Taro asked about parking and received information on where they could put the Jeep for the night. He stuffed the receipt in his wallet with the credit card. "We'll be back in just a minute," he said to the clerk. "We have to move the car over and bring in our luggage."

"Very good, sir," the clerk said again. He gave Taro a parking permit for the hotel garage, and added, "We hope you have a pleasant stay."

"Are you really sure you want to do this?" she whispered. "This place must be expensive."

He smiled. "So? This has been a perfect day. Let's end it with a perfect night."

Chapter 12

A huge lodge pole bed took center stage in their luxurious, western-themed suite. Far off to the side were matching dressers, a table and chairs, and a fully-stocked bar in a sideboard.

"Wow! This is really something. Kind of wild west deluxe," Gina commented.

Taro laughed, taking it all in. "I almost expect to see John Wayne show up at any minute."

She made a face. "Well, let's hope not. I don't want to share this with anyone but you."

* * *

In a separate section of the room, a giant heart-shaped bathtub beckoned. They soaked together in a sea of bubbles and drank the complimentary champagne.

Taro sighed in contentment. "This is really nice. I have never been in a bath like this, with all these bubbles. In Japan, we usually wash our bodies first, and rinse off the soap before we get into the bath. That way the water stays clean. We also have public baths, so more than one person can take a bath together."

"You mean taking a bath with other people?"

"Yeah."

"Really? How many others?"

"Oh, sometimes a lot."

"What? Are you serious? Being naked in a bath with a bunch of strangers?"

"Yeah. We don't feel embarrassed about being naked like Americans seem to."

Gina's mouth dropped open.

"Everyone has a body, so what's the big deal?" He shrugged. "Nobody stares at anyone else. That's not polite. People pretty much keep to themselves. It's a good place to relax and think."

"Wow. I think that would take some getting used to…"

"Don't worry," he soothed. "Men and women usually have separate areas."

"Oh."

"But, there are some places where men and women can bathe together. Mostly families, but sometimes couples."

"But they're in there with a bunch of other couples?"

"Well, yes, sometimes, but no one looks at anyone else."

She was silent as she considered this.

Taro added, "But this is nice. The soapy water feels good. Very relaxing."

He stretched out, flexing his toes. "Very relaxing," he said again.

When they climbed out of the tub, Taro bundled her up in one of the oversized towels and moved with her to the bed. He unwrapped the towel and lay down at her side.

"I want to kiss you everywhere," he whispered, leaning over her and kissing her forehead, down her nose to her neck. His kisses turned into licks as he moved down her body, tasting her skin as he went. He licked the insides of her thighs down to her feet, then came back up again to her thighs. "And I want to taste your wetness. I want to taste what you feel like when I come into you."

His words came as a shock, but she hardly had time to process what he had said before his wet mouth closed on her and his warm tongue pushed into her most private flesh.

"M-mmmm," he said, looking up at her with a smile. "I like it."

She felt her face redden all the way down her neck.

"Don't be embarrassed," he continued. "It is natural. And I can tell you like it, too. You are already wet for me."

Gina was so embarrassed she almost choked, but she raised her eyes to meet his. "I can't help it. You have that effect on me."

"That's good," he whispered. His tongue pushed into her again, this time pulsing in and out and around.

Oh my God, I'm melting inside. She panted with need.

Taro's eyes locked with hers as he moved over her and replaced his tongue with his hardened length, pushing all the way into her. He gripped her hips with his hands, pulling her up to meet his thrusts, then suddenly flipped her over onto her stomach and inserted a pillow beneath her. He pulled her bottom up higher and plunged into her again and again with more vigorous thrusting and even deeper penetration.

Oh my God. It feels so good this way—I'm on the edge, I'm falling, falling, spiraling out into space, falling into him.

Gina panted as she tried to meet his thrusts with her own motions. She heard him moan, then he increased the tempo until she was unable to keep up. She surrendered to the waves of pleasure washing over her until everything around her exploded into bits of light. She cried out as he brought her to the most shattering orgasm she had ever known. She heard him call her name, and then he collapsed over her, spent. They lay together for a long time before they could breathe again normally.

Taro rolled over to her side and pulled her back to him so they were facing each other. He gazed at her with his eyes half closed.

They lay in each other's arms, basking in the afterglow, until Taro said, "Hey, Moonstorm, I think it's time to sleep now." He leaned over and kissed her. "Good night, Gina. Sweet dreams."

"Good night, Taro," she whispered. "See you in the morning."

The room grew quiet except for the sounds of their breathing, and the gurgling sounds of the creek flowing below their balcony. The atmosphere was tranquil and peaceful. *Very Zen.* The full moon outside was the only illumination in the room.

"Taro?" Gina asked softly.

No reply.

Gina leaned closer. "You make me feel beautiful," she confided in a whisper. She kissed his cheek and settled herself next to him.

She awakened once during the night, appreciating the liquid sounds of the creek and the rays of moonlight stretching across the room. Cold air wafted in from windows they had left open to the balcony, contrasting with the comforting warmth of Taro's body next to her. She sighed in blissful happiness and moved closer to him. They snuggled together under the fluffy duvet that covered them, wrapping them together.

* * *

Breakfast the next morning was served on the balcony, brought up by two waiters from room service. A feast was laid out, including steaming platters of scrambled eggs, ham and bacon, a basket of assorted muffins with fresh butter, sliced strawberries and pineapple on a silver tray, a carafe of orange juice, a pot of wonderful smelling coffee with a pitcher of cream, and an arrangement of fresh flowers.

"Wow, this really is a fancy place," Gina said, gesturing to the breakfast selections and the matching, fluffy robes furnished by the hotel. "First class. I didn't really get to see much of it last night. I seemed to be…busy."

Taro bit back a laugh. "I'm glad we stayed here instead of trying to drive back last night. This has been a lot more fun. Besides, we needed to do something special to celebrate."

"That's really sweet of you," Gina mumbled, feeling a blush begin to burn on her cheeks.

They ate in silence for a time.

"I'm curious about your name." He reached for a muffin and buttered it. "It's Italian, isn't it?"

"Yes. My grandmother wanted to give me a special name, since I was the only girl in the family. She came up with Gina, for Gina Lollobrigida, who was a popular movie star in the sixties. She was very beautiful and glamorous. I guess she thought that giving me that name would make me beautiful and glamorous, too."

"You are beautiful," Taro said, nuzzling her cheek. "Do you have a middle name?"

"Marie. After my grandmother."

"That's nice. So your name is Gina Marie. I like it." He took a bite of his muffin.

"What about your name—Taro? Does it have a meaning?"

"First-born son. It's a very typical Japanese name for boys. There must be thousands of Taros in Japan."

"Maybe. But there couldn't be another one like you."

"My family name is Mori. It means forest."

He leaned closer and tilted his head as he gazed into her eyes. "Your eyes are so green. So interesting—I feel like I could get lost looking in them. I've never known anyone with eyes that color before."

"And yours are so dark, so mysterious. Not like anyone I've ever known. Fascinating."

"Maybe," he laughed. "But if you were in Japan, you would see a lot of eyes like mine."

"Still," she smiled. "I think they're beautiful."

* * *

The rest of the week passed much too fast but it was the happiest week Gina could remember. She and Taro grew closer. *And the nights were unbelievable.*

Chapter 13

Phoenix

THE MORNING when Taro had to leave, Gina was quiet as she drank her coffee, trying to think of what to say. Conflicting thoughts rumbled through her mind like an approaching thundercloud. Would she see him again after today? Their time together had been more than wonderful, but was this all they would have? Old insecurities surfaced as she considered the idea that maybe all of this had been nothing more than a nice diversion for him, and he would soon return to his world, leaving her behind. *So, what happens now?* She wanted to ask him, but could not allow herself to risk the possible rejection the question might bring.

He was still packing upstairs. "Quit fretting!" she told herself and walked into the kitchen to make breakfast. She quickly scrambled some eggs and made toast. "Taro," she called as she poured a cup of coffee for him. "Breakfast is ready."

Taro clumped down the stairs wearing his new cowboy boots, carrying his suitcase. He placed it by the door and joined her in the kitchen.

"Mmmmmm," he said as he bent to her with a quick kiss. He took a sip of coffee. "Good. Thanks for making breakfast. It will be a long flight."

She pointed to his boots. "Do you think you'll be comfortable wearing those all day?"

He glanced down at the boots. "I hope so. Besides, there was not enough room in the suitcase for them."

She almost suggested that he could come back for them later, but hesitated. *I don't want him to think that I'm expecting anything from him. If he comes back, I want it to be because he wants to. If this is to be a break, it should be a clean one.*

Taro glanced at the clock. "We should leave soon. I don't want to miss the flight."

A sense of gloom descended on her, almost a confirmation of her fears. She managed to smile. "All right."

"I know you have to get to work, so just let me out in front of the airport. You don't have to go inside with me."

Is he being considerate, or just typically Japanese about not showing affection in public? If he is anxious to leave, maybe this is better. If I was in the terminal with him I'd never want to let him go.

She drove to Sky Harbor and pulled into the 'Departures' lane in front of Terminal 4. Posted signs advised drivers to stay in their cars, or get a ticket. Several uniformed traffic officers busied themselves with keeping the traffic moving.

Taro read one of the signs out loud. "Do Not Park. Violators will be ticketed." He turned to her. "I should get out now."

He opened the door, got out, grabbed his suitcase from the back, then leaned to her with a kiss.

"I don't want to leave, but I have to get back to New York. Then we go on the road."

Gina's thoughts were in a turmoil. *So, is this the end?*

Taro gazed into her eyes as if he understood exactly what she was feeling. "I will call you when I get back tonight," he promised.

"Okay," she whispered.

"I don't know exactly when, but when we get back out west, maybe we can meet in one of the cities where we have a show. How would you feel about that?"

"Sure. That would be great," she replied. *What a lame thing to say—like some kind of automated response.*

He smiled. "Good. Let's try to do that then. I'll call you tonight." He leaned in for another kiss, then pulled away and shut the door.

She watched as he turned and walked into the terminal, and soon he was no longer visible. Suddenly it was too quiet. The Jeep felt empty; all warmth gone as if he took it with him when he left.

Gina sighed, shifted gears, and pulled away from the curb. "Time to get back to the real world," she commanded herself as she drove away from the airport and back to her job. That was her reality. *But, Taro is real, too, and the time I spent with him is also reality.* Tears stung her eyes. She missed him already.

At the store, she struggled to focus. After a while, being back in her familiar world occupied her thoughts. She settled into her accustomed rhythm, and the morning passed.

Lynn joined her at the table for lunch. "What's wrong?" she asked. "You look distracted."

"What's right?" Gina sighed. "Not much; not right at this moment."

Lynn looked alarmed. "What do you mean?"

"Nothing," Gina forced a smile. "Everything's fine."

"It doesn't look like it."

"Leave it alone, Lynn."

"Okay, but you look sad. Any problems with you and the Japanese guy?"

"No. He's fine."

Comprehension flashed in Lynn's eyes. "But he must have left, huh? When?"

"This morning."

"Okay. That explains it. So, how was everything?"

"Wonderful," Gina groaned. "Just wonderful."

"But he had to leave."

"Yeah."

"And you're wondering if you'll see him again and what will happen." Gina nodded.

Lynn met Gina's eyes. "I know how that is. Believe me, I understand. But it went well? For him, too?"

Gina nodded again. "I think so."

"Well, all I can say is that if it's meant to be, things will find a way to work out," Lynn soothed, tucking an arm around Gina's shoulders. "At least you got to meet him like you wanted and a chance to be with him like you wanted. No matter what else happens, you will have your memories, and nothing can take that away."

"I know," Gina agreed. "At least I have that."

"So, you have a reason to smile. And, I predict you'll hear from him. Yeah, I do," she confirmed as she saw Gina's head snap up. "Meanwhile, welcome back to your life."

"Lynn's right," Gina said to herself throughout the afternoon. *Some things are either on, or off and can't be forced. Still…*

* * *

At home, many hours later, after several unsuccessful attempts to interest herself in a television movie, Gina picked up a magazine. She read and re-read the same page several times, but could not remember what the article was about.

Taro had not called, and the silence hung in the room like a cold fog.

Gina decided to go upstairs to bed. In the bathroom, she brushed her teeth, catching a glimpse of her reflection in the mirror. "Stop this!" she addressed the worried face that gazed back at her. "I'm sure there is a perfectly good reason why he hasn't called."

She ambled into the bedroom, kicked off her slippers, and clambered into bed. The sheets felt cold.

"Come, Cheddar," she called.

Cheddar stared at Gina with big round eyes, but did not move from her position across the room.

"Oh, for Pete's sake!" Gina snapped. She threw the covers aside, marched across the room, and scooped the cat up in her arms. She returned to bed and snuggled against the soft fur, but Cheddar slithered out of Gina's clutches and bolted to the foot of the bed.

"What's wrong with you?" Gina sat up and reached for the elusive cat, who managed to avoid her.

As Gina reached toward Cheddar again, the phone rang.

For a moment she froze, then she vaulted out of bed and yanked up the receiver.

"Hi." Taro's voice sounded on the line. "Sorry to call so late, but it was a long trip and I've been busy since I got back."

"That's all right. How are you?"

"Tired. There was a long delay in Chicago, and after I got back, I was in meetings about the tour. Then Chazz wanted to go over some new stuff, and that took some time. This is the first chance I have had to call you."

He yawned. "I need to sleep."

There was a moment of silence, and then he added, "It would be nice to have you here."

Gina felt her pulse quicken. "And it would be nice if you were still here."

"Yeah. That would be good." He sighed. "I have to go but I wanted you to know I'm back, like I promised. I will try to call you tomorrow."

"I miss talking to you," Gina admitted.

"Me, too."

"Good night, Taro."

"Good night." She heard him hang up.

Gina stretched and looked around. Was it her imagination, or did she feel warmer now? She glanced toward her bed, where Cheddar lay curled up like a ball next to her pillow.

Chapter 14

March—Seattle

"Taro, you won't believe this, but I'll be in Seattle for about a week next month! La Mode is launching a new store up there, and some of us are going up to help with the Grand Opening."

"Really? That's great news! We will be in Seattle sometime next month, too. We will have to find a way to get together."

Four months had passed since Taro's visit. During that time Moonstorm had been touring, including back in Japan. Phone calls between them had been irregular, but he had even managed to call her for Christmas.

Sometimes she wondered if they would eventually run out of things to say, but so far that had not happened. There was always so much to share about what they were doing while apart that there was always something new to talk about.

But what happens now? After four months apart, will we still feel the same attraction?

* * *

Gina and Lynn flew into Sea-Tac Airport with the Phoenix group, where they were picked up by a hotel shuttle. They barely had time to freshen up before they were whisked to the new store for a meeting.

"Look at all the celebrities here," Lynn whispered. "There's David Rosenberg, the Regional Manager, and two of the DuVall sons, plus some models and fashion designers, some media people, and a bunch of other people I've never seen before."

Introductions were made, pictures were taken, and assignments were given for handling a host of special events, prize drawings, and demonstrations that would be offered to the public.

Gina was assigned to a group of new hires, explaining what was expected from them during the grand opening, stressing the importance of keeping all the display tables and racks looking neat and stocked. A number of 'free gift with purchase' items were located throughout the store, and instructions were issued about how to manage these promotions.

At one o'clock in the afternoon, the store officially opened, complete with a visit by the mayor, television crews, a ribbon-cutting, and finally, an invitation to the waiting spectators to enter. A large crowd surged through the doors and scattered throughout the store.

The day passed in a blur as Gina assisted customers and salespeople, checked stock levels on display tables, answered questions, and multiple other duties.

When it was time to return to the hotel, Gina realized she was exhausted. "I was so busy today I didn't even have time to eat lunch," she complained.

Lynn nodded in agreement. "Yeah, I know. I'm bushed. It's been a really long day, and my face hurts from having to smile so much."

"Me, too. And my feet are killing me from having to wear these high heels all day."

As soon as she reached her room, Gina checked her phone. *Nothing yet from Taro.* She sighed. *I wish I could hear his voice.* She wondered when he would arrive in town.

The next day was hectic, but passed smoothly. Several cartons of new stock had been delivered in her area. Gina worked with the salespeople, showing them how to check in the merchandise, and helping them get it out on the selling floor as soon as possible.

Upon her return to her room that night, her heartbeat ratcheted up when she noticed the red message light was blinking.

She picked up the phone and listened to a message from Taro, saying he would call again later, and that he would be in town the next day.

Late in the night, the phone rang. Taro's voice came through, sweet and clear. "So sorry to call this late, but we just finished a show. I'll be in Seattle sometime tomorrow. We will be in rehearsal all afternoon. Then we have a show. I'll take a taxi to your hotel after that."

"Sounds good. I'll leave an envelope for you at the front desk with a key. Then you can just come up whenever you get here."

She imagined she could hear a smile in his voice when he replied, "Okay. I really want to see you. It has been a long time."

"Yes, it has," she agreed. *Four months.* "I'll see you tomorrow night, then."

"Tomorrow night," he confirmed, and hung up the phone.

* * *

After their third day of the Grand Opening, Gina and Lynn sat together on the shuttle back to the hotel, laughing as Lynn made jokes about shooting some of the obnoxious customers she had to deal with that day.

Gina decided to take a long soak in the tub, using some of the body wash she received as part of a new fragrance introduction. She toweled herself off and slipped on her nightgown, then got into bed, intending to read while she waited for Taro.

She awakened to the rustling sound of the sheets being pulled aside. Taro settled against her back, kissing her shoulder.

"Hi," he whispered.

"Taro?" she sighed. "Is it really you, or am I dreaming?"

"No, It's me. Sorry to be so late. I got here as soon as I could," he whispered, kissing her. Gina could taste tobacco and alcohol on his tongue, and there was a trace of stubble on his face.

"She yawned. "I must have fallen asleep. I didn't even hear you come in."

He chuckled. "Well, I didn't want to waste any time," he whispered, nuzzling her cheek. He kissed her nose and moved across to her ear with kisses. He took a deep breath, inhaling her scent.

"Mmmmm, you smell even better than usual," he breathed.

"Oh. We all got samples of a new fragrance we just introduced at the store. It's called 'Impulse'. If you really like it, I'll have to buy some."

He nuzzled her neck, closing his eyes and sniffing, then opened his eyes and winked at her. "Yeah, I like it. Really nice," he said in a low, husky tone.

She rolled over to look directly into his eyes. "Have I ever told you that you have a sexy voice?"

"You think so?"

"Yeah. Your voice is very melodious, kind of musical. Very sexy."

He looked somewhat flustered. "Well, I'm glad you like my voice. What about the rest of me?"

"Oh, that," she teased, peering at him with one eye closed. She flashed him an appraising look. "That's pretty sexy, too."

He laughed. "I think I should take a shower. It's been a long day."

"Sure. Go ahead."

A few minutes later, Taro had disappeared into the bathroom and thrown his clothes out onto the floor, and then she heard the sound of water running. She smiled as she listened to him humming amid the sounds of splashing.

The water stopped. He walked back into the room, covered only by a towel he had wrapped around his waist. He picked up his clothes from the floor and hung them up, then turned to her, tilting his head to the side

"Listen," he said. "Can you hear it? It's raining."

"Is it?"

Taro walked to the window, opened the curtains, and looked out, his shape in silhouette against the lights from outside. He pushed the sliding glass door all the way open, to the pinging sound of rain hitting the balcony floor. "He turned back to her. Do you hear it now?"

"Yeah. And I love it. When you live in the desert, the sound of rain is like heaven."

"*So desu.* Rain makes everything smell so clean. Like the earth is washing itself," he mused. "Did you know that in Japanese, the word for 'pretty' and 'clean' is the same? *Kirei.*"

"No, I didn't know that, but I think it's interesting. Like you. You're interesting."

He walked back to her, threw off the towel, climbed into bed, and nestled next to her. "Let's see what else you think is interesting," he said, grinning and pulling the covers up and over them.

"I have missed you, Taro," she whispered.

"And I have missed you."

She sighed, enjoying the feeling of Taro's warm silky skin against hers. They lay together, with her head on his chest, looking out at the view, listening to the rain. For a long time, there was no other sound in the room. Sweetness seemed to float in the air around them, filling the room.

"This is so peaceful," she whispered. "And look, out there, where the lights stop. That's Puget Sound. It's beautiful. All that water, with mountains on the other side.

"The air here smells so fresh," he said. "Let's leave the window open all night."

"I'd like that. And maybe in the morning we can take the ferry across, before I have to go to work."

"What if it's raining?" he asked.

She turned to him with a kiss. "That's what hair dryers are for."

Taro smiled and pulled her closer, opening the little buttons on the front of her gown. He tugged at the fabric until it slipped away from her and began kissing her now bare arms and shoulders.

She sighed, enjoying the delicious sensation of his hands stroking her body. She could feel his swelling erection pushing urgently against her thigh.

He reached between her legs, pulling off her panties. His erection was now very hard, almost painful, as he pressed against her. Keeping his hands between her legs, he extended his fingers up and into her very gently, stroking and caressing her.

Her breath caught in her throat and a warm thick wetness began forming within her, oozing out onto his fingers.

He moaned and wrapped his arms around her, holding her hips tightly against his body, and she felt his hardness enter her, pushing all the way in. The intensity made her gasp in surprise.

He stopped. "Am I hurting you?" he asked anxiously. His length was warm within her, filling her. When he spoke, his words vibrated through him, including that part of him deep inside her. It was a strange sensation, but she liked it.

"No," she whispered. "Don't stop. You feel so good." She enclosed his hands in hers. "Make love to me."

He emitted a kind of groaning noise as he began to move within her, pulling her into a position where her hips were almost at a right angle with his body and his penetration was deep.

She could hardly breathe as wave after wave of unbelievable pleasure swept over her. She heard herself her cry out and pushed harder against his body. His hands gripped her even tighter against him as he moved within her.

In a blurry mist, she felt herself floating, up into a heaven of the senses. All awareness of anything else faded away. There was nothing else except now, and the union they shared.

* * *

Sometime in the middle of the night Gina awakened. Rain was still falling. She slowly pulled away from Taro, stood up and walked to the window, looking out into the night, breathing the fresh, cold air.

Behind her, she heard Taro call her name. "You must be cold. Come back in here with me and get warm." He held his arms open for her, and pulled the covers up over them as she snuggled against his chest.

"Mmmmmm. The air is crispy, and you're so warm. A perfect combination."

"Yes. Perfect," he agreed. He wrapped his arms around her and pulled her closer.

She sighed with contentment and settled against him like two spoons nesting together. He kissed her shoulder. "Maybe we should try to sleep," he suggested. "We both had a long day."

She yawned and sighed again. "Yes, maybe we should. Besides, we still have tomorrow."

* * *

"Taro! Come look out the window. It's beautiful."

He stood by her side as they admired the view. The rain had stopped. Against a sky of pale blue, clusters of low clouds hung over the water. Crests of blue-shaded mountains peeked out above, some tipped with white from a recent snow. The whole scene was bathed in watercolor shades of blue, peaceful and serene.

They took a ferry across to Bremerton, standing together outside the cabin, against the railing. She leaned her head back against him. His coat was open, wrapped around her with his arms inside. The warmth of his body contrasted with the cold, fresh air around them. A few people were also out on the deck, but paid them no attention. Another couple stood together wrapped in each other's arms. *Like lovers. Like us.*

Remembering their time commitments, they remained on the ferry for the return trip back to Seattle, enjoying a spectacular view of the city skyline with Mt. Rainer towering in the background.

"It looks a little like Mount Fuji, doesn't it?" she teased.

"A bit." He kissed her hair. "It is really beautiful here."

They shared an early lunch with fresh-caught salmon, and gazed out over the sound, now filled with boats.

A short taxi ride took them back to the hotel. Gina noticed with relief that none of the La Mode people were in the lobby. They took the elevator up to Gina's room for some time together before she had to meet the afternoon shuttle.

She rushed to get dressed, kissed Taro good-bye and hurried down to the lobby.

Gina caught a glimpse of her reflection in the elevator door. *I look so happy. And, there's still tonight. Tomorrow we will both have to leave Seattle. But we still have tonight. I can wake up tomorrow in his arms again.* She winked at her reflection.

Lynn would never guess that Taro was there, in the hotel, since she had had no idea that his band was in town. *Good. She doesn't need to know.* Taro would leave later, long after the shuttle had departed, so there was no chance that she would ever know. By the time he returned to her after his show, Lynn would already be asleep.

* * *

It was late when Gina and Lynn returned to the hotel, since this time they had to close the store before they could leave.

Gina yawned. "I had been thinking it would be nice to go get a drink or something, but I'm just too tired."

"Yeah, me too," Lynn agreed. "I'm exhausted. This event has worn me out. I can't wait to get home tomorrow."

"I'm worn out, too," Gina said. "Let's get together when we get back home, all right?"

"Sure. Well, good night," Lynn yawned and headed toward her room.

"Good night," Gina called. "See you in the morning."

Well, she's right about being tired, but I'm not worn out. Yet. By tomorrow I will be, though, after another night with Taro. By tomorrow, I'll probably be exhausted, but it'll be worth it. Tonight is our last night together for God knows how long, and I'm sure he will absolutely wear me out. He'll be tired tomorrow, too. Maybe we can both sleep on the trip out of town.

Her pulse raced at this thought and realized she was grinning. *He is so hot. Lord help me, he turns me on so much. And I love every minute of it.*

She took a shower and decided to wait up for him, sitting in a chair watching television. Before long, she fell asleep despite herself, but awakened when she felt his arms around her and his lips on hers.

"Oh!" she said, startled. "I was waiting for you but I must have fallen asleep."

"That's all right," he said between kisses. "I'm sure you had a busy day, and we didn't get much sleep last night." He grinned. "I don't think we'll get much sleep tonight, either."

"I was just thinking the same thing," she teased. "How did the show go tonight?"

"Good."

"I'm glad," she said.

"But, I just wanted it to be over so I could be back here with you."

"Really?"

"Yeah. After tonight, it will be a long time before I can see you again."

"I know," she whispered.

"Earlier today, I was listening to an old EZO song called 'Million Miles Away'. That's exactly how I feel when we are not together. Loneliness that won't fade away. It's a good song. And now, I'll be on the road for months, away from you. But, as soon as I can, I will come back to Phoenix and you. Maybe in June, okay?"

"I would like that. It's only a few months from now."

What she did not say was how being with him again, even for this short time, reinforced her feeling that she would always want to be with him. She was thrilled at the thought that he seemed to feel the same way.

* * *

Morning came much too soon, and Gina was a few minutes late in meeting the shuttle group in the lobby. She sat next to Lynn and looked out the window, closed her eyes and remembered the look on Taro's face when they said their good-byes. She focused her thoughts on the way he held her face in both his hands when he kissed her, and she sighed.

Lynn glanced at her and yawned. "Tonight we'll be back home," she said.

That afternoon, on the flight back to Phoenix, Gina inquired, "Hey, Lynn, are you planning to use that sample of 'Impulse' they gave us?"

"Yeah. Why?"

"Oh, just wondering. I may have to buy some."

"What? You never buy perfume. What's up?"

"I like it."

"And…?" Lynn arched her eyebrows, waiting.

Gina blushed.

Lynn narrowed her eyes. "Okay, Gina, what have you been up to? Did you meet someone in Seattle?"

Gina hesitated. "Well…"

Lynn's eyes flew open. "Oh, my God, don't tell me. Was he up there, too?"

"Yeah," Gina confessed in a whisper. "He had a show. We got together after that."

"In the hotel?"

"Yeah."

"No wonder you were in such a hurry to get back to your room!" Lynn snorted.

"It was only two nights."

"Yeah. Only two nights. So, now what?"

"He's on the road. He said something about coming back to Phoenix in June."

"And you're thinking about buying perfume?"

"He likes it."

"Dear Lord, Gina, you're crazy!"

"Yeah, I know. And I love it." She yawned.

Lynn rolled her eyes. "You didn't get much sleep, did you?"

"No," Gina admitted and smiled.

Chapter 15

June—Phoenix

IN LATE JUNE, Moonstorm was still on tour, playing in clubs around the country, sometimes opening for a hot new band called Hammersmith. During a break in the tour, Taro flew back to Phoenix.

Gina's schedule was erratic due to special store events around the 4th of July holiday. "Don't worry," Taro assured her. "I just want to relax. We have toured so much I need some quiet time. We can work around your schedule and stay close to home."

This plan worked remarkably well, and Gina was amazed by how naturally they seemed to fit back together, even after a separation. On days when she was at work, Taro hiked the mountain trails behind her house or stayed at home, and they enjoyed catching up at dinnertime. They took day trips when they could, including another trip to Sedona with more of her jewelry. On mornings when they could sleep late, they stayed in bed, enjoying the luxury of relaxing together, slipping in and out of sleep.

One such morning, Gina was tempted to take the day off. Taro, however, thought it was important that she keep to her schedule.

"It's so Japanese of you to be so concerned with work," she complained. She shot him a wicked look.

He laughed. "I don't want to be the reason for you being late, or anything else that could make problems for you," he declared with finality.

"But I don't want to go in today," she pouted. "It's really hard to be there when I would rather be here with you. Really hard."

He pulled her closer and placed her hand on the front of his jeans. "It's always hard when you're close to me," he teased.

Gina giggled. She did not move her hand away, stroking him gently, appreciating his warmth and the feeling of him growing harder under her fingers. "Mmmm," she breathed and looked up into his eyes. She reached for the top of his zipper.

As usual, he seemed to know exactly what she was thinking. He grinned and bent to kiss her nose. "Later," he breathed into her ear. "Let's wait for tonight. Right now you have to leave for work."

And so, she left for the store, but thinking of that exchange made her smile all the way there.

The first person Gina encountered when she arrived was Jamie, her new assistant.

Jamie frowned. "The Weasel was just here. We have a visit from Bernice Goldman, the representative from Wishing Star Jewelry today! I'm nervous. Aren't you?"

Gina set down her briefcase. "No, not really. Why?"

"Well, I've heard she's a tough cookie and she got a manager at one of the other stores fired."

Gina laughed. "I heard that, too, when I was new here. But I made sure everything in the department looked great, and I was prepared when she got here. She liked what she saw, and over the last two years, we've gotten to be friends. "So, I'm not stressed about today."

"Really? You like her?"

"Yes, I do. The same thing could happen with any of our vendors, you know. If they aren't happy with the way their merchandise is presented, they can complain and cause a lot of trouble. They have a right to be concerned with their image—it is their brand, after all. I've found the best way to impress someone like Bernice is to be a good merchandiser. You know, showing off their products to the best advantage. That's what gets the customer's attention and drives sales. And this business is all about sales. I don't think we have to worry."

"Okay, Gina." Jamie looked relieved. "I'll go check all the display cases again, and make sure all the back stock is in the right place."

"That sounds great, Jamie. Thank you!"

Jamie rushed out and Gina noticed Lynn walking in. "Vendor visit?" she asked.

"Yeah, Bernice from Wishing Star. She has a reputation of being hard to please."

"I've heard that, too," Lynn agreed. "But some of the designers are much worse. Lots of overstuffed egos to deal with."

"Yeah, no kidding," Gina agreed. "Some of them have such big heads it's a wonder they can fit through the door!"

The two friends exchanged a look and laughed.

"I'll leave you to it, then," Lynn said and went out, leaving Gina alone in her office.

Gina recalled the first time she met Bernice, back when she had been a new department manager.

Bernice was short and plump, extremely well-dressed in what was most certainly a designer suit, her silver hair smartly styled, giving her a much younger appearance than a woman in her late fifties. She was "all business" at first, but warmed up as she inspected the displays. Gina had placed the jewelry collections where they would get maximum exposure to customers and generate the highest sales. At the end of the visit, Bernice had nothing but praise for Gina and her department.

"I must admit that I didn't expect this level of professionalism from a new manager," Bernice had said. That was the beginning of a relationship that had grown over the next several years.

* * *

Today, when Bernice arrived, she walked through Gina's department, checking display cases and counters. "As usual, Gina, your department looks great," Bernice purred. "It's no wonder your sales are the best in the division."

"Thanks, Bernice. That means a lot to me. We try hard to make you smile every time you come in."

"And you do, Gina. It's obvious that you train your people well. Everything is in order, neat and clean, and your displays really show off our collections. Why don't we talk some more over lunch? I have some news."

They strolled out into the mall to the food court, picked a table and sat down.

Bernice began, "Gina, we're introducing a vintage collection called 'Heirloom Treasures'. Our marketing is telling us that women like things that look like pieces passed down. It's kind of a nostalgic, romantic look. And we want to test it in your store first."

Gina blinked in surprise. "Wow, Bernice. I'm flattered."

Bernice smiled. "I thought you'd be happy. We're on track to launch in early November."

"Perfect timing," Gina said. "Just before the holidays."

"Exactly," Bernice smiled and patted Gina's hand. "Now, let's catch up on other things."

Bernice chatted about a trip she and her husband were planning to take to the Holy Land in the next month, and shared funny stories of other travels they had taken. She took a long sip of her iced tea and gazed at Gina thoughtfully.

"I must say, Gina, you seem different somehow today. You look happier than I've ever seen you." She paused. "Is there someone new in your life?"

Gina stared down at the table and blushed.

"I thought so," Bernice observed with a shrewd glance. "Good for you. I'd love to see you happy with someone. Don't let yourself get so busy with your career you don't make time for a relationship."

Gina smiled. "That's good advice."

Bernice continued, "Believe me, Gina, a good relationship is worth everything, and I should know. It's the way my marriage has always been. Ira and I were high school sweethearts. We married for love, and we're still in love today, even after all these years. At first, my parents didn't approve. He didn't get good grades in school, so they thought he'd never amount to much. But in college, he got interested in finance, and he's been one of the most successful accountants in the country for years." She paused and took another bite of her salad. "So, you can't always know how things will turn out."

"Thanks, Bernice. I really don't know what will happen," Gina confided. "We're still too new. But he's not like anyone else I've ever known. Our backgrounds are completely different, but it feels like we belong together. Everything seems to click."

Bernice smiled. "Well, then, enjoy it. Don't lose it. Love is what makes life worth living."

* * *

That night, Taro took Gina to see some new bands at a local club. One of them was a young Japanese band. They played well, but the crowd was noisy, rude and drunk. They heard some catcalls of 'Go back to Japan!' that were probably an attempt at humor.

Taro was visibly upset. He sat stiffly in his chair in deadly silence, his lips firmed into a tight line, his eyes narrowed, and drank more than she had ever seen him do before.

He was silent all the way home. Gina decided to leave him alone with his thoughts while she drove. Once they were back in the house, she ventured that she had enjoyed the band, but thought the audience was extremely rude.

"I've had things like that happen to me before!" he erupted. "Sometimes Americans can be really insulting—and mean!"

He stomped to the refrigerator and fished out a beer, opened it, then turned to look at her. She could tell he was leading up to something and it would be explosive.

"Do you Americans think we feel nothing? He thundered in his frustration and pain. "You think we don't have feelings, just like you?"

Gina sat in silence, trying to give him space to vent.

He glanced over at her. "We love, hope, dream, grieve for those we loved and lost, just like you."

He lit a cigarette and was quiet for a moment, then continued, "I cried at the deaths of Taiji and Munetaka and Hide...so much light, gone out of this world forever. And they were not even known here."

He blew out a long breath of smoke. "America is such a big country, but is so self-absorbed. A lot of Americans don't want to check out culture from other places, because you think it could not possibly be as good. Do you know how much that hurts?" He finished the beer and smacked the empty can down on the table.

He took several more drags on his cigarette while he collected his thoughts.

"It's not fair, really," he muttered, and put out the cigarette. "All we want is an equal chance. If we were British or Australian, our music would be accepted right away because Americans would think we *looked like them*. They could identify with us. They don't usually feel that way when they find out we are Japanese. If they know that ahead of time, some people don't even want to hear us."

He opened another beer, then walked over to the sofa and flopped down. "Sometimes I think coming to America is like a ship that gets wrecked on the rocks before it reaches the harbor. Impossible to get in." He paused to light another cigarette.

"It has really been difficult for us. Some people look at us, our eyes," he said, gesturing to his own, "and they think 'Those damned Japs'. They don't always say it, but I can still feel it."

A stab of pain shot through Gina as she tried to imagine being in Taro's situation.

"At a club in Texas once, after a show, some guys called us sneaky Japs and shouted things like 'remember Pearl Harbor!' We almost got into a fight, but the club security broke it up."

He paused again and glanced at her. "How long will people here hate us for what happened so long ago? They forget you bombed my country, too, and not just military areas. What about Hiroshima? What about Nagasaki?" he grimaced bitterly. "My father's uncle died when a bomb hit a school building. He was a teacher, not involved with the war at all."

Aurora Dawning

"But all that happened a long time before I was born." He sighed and put out the last of his cigarette.

Taro suddenly looked exhausted. He reached for another cigarette and lit it, watching the smoke slowly float away as he exhaled.

She walked across to sit beside him, reaching for his hand.

He turned to her and sighed again. "I am talking too much," he said quietly.

"I don't think so," she soothed. I never realized before how hard it has been for you, but you should know that not all Americans feel like that."

There was no answer to this. She squeezed his hand and continued, "Taro, I do understand how you feel, and you are right. I think music is a kind of universal language. It can help all of us learn from each other."

His head jerked up.

"And I will always want to hear how you feel. "

They sat together in silence for a few minutes.

He spoke quietly, reaching from far within himself for the right words to say.

She listened, understanding that he was trusting her with his feelings. She could feel his pain, his frustration, and she understood everything. It was as if she had fallen into his world. What he felt, she felt. What he saw, she also saw.

He stopped talking and looked at her.

"Taro, do you remember the first time you were here when you told me about some Japanese bands you liked? Remember, you talked about X-Japan, EZO, and Loudness?"

He nodded.

"When you first told me about them, I had no idea who they were, but after that I looked them up and listened to their music. You were right. They're all great. And, I know who you are talking about; Hide, Taiji, and Munetaka. All three of them were exceptional. They were truly gifted; and all of them left us too soon.

He stared at her in surprise as she continued, "You are right to be sad about that. It is true that so much light went out of the world when they died, but did you ever think that their light helped show you the way; that they led the way for you to follow? Do you think they would be happy if you just gave up?"

He looked startled. "No."

"That's right. You owe it to their memory to keep going. You can live for them. You have to live not only for you but for them, because they no longer can."

He sat in silence as he considered this.

After a while, he spoke again. "I am drinking too much," he stated softly. "I am sorry."

"I'm more worried about your smoking too much," she pointed out. "Those things will kill you, and I wouldn't like that."

He put out the cigarette and stared at her.

"Come on to bed," she suggested in a quiet voice. "You need to rest."

She helped him upstairs to the bedroom and managed to get his boots off before he swayed and fell over onto the bed. She covered him with a blanket and crawled in next to him.

That night he slept apart from her. Gina woke in the middle of the night, feeling cold without his warmth wrapped around her. It seemed strange, but at least he was with her, not out driving somewhere. He was safe here and could sleep off the effects of the alcohol.

Sometime just before dawn he awakened, still wearing all his clothes. She felt him pull her closer and wrap his arms around her. Then he sighed and drifted back into sleep.

* * *

Later that morning, Taro woke up again, alone in the room. He wondered where Gina was, and thought back to the night before.

It feels like a hammer pounding in my head—too much to drink last night. I should not have let myself get so angry. I need coffee. Lots of coffee. Hangover. Apology.

He rolled over to the edge of the bed and wobbled to his feet. "Gina?" he called.

"I'm down here."

He walked downstairs to the kitchen. She was sitting at the table reading the newspaper.

"Well, you're awake!" she teased and put the paper down.

"Yeah, I'm awake." He held his head. "Not sure if I'm alive. My head hurts."

He cast her a quick glance before he continued. "I am sorry for last night. I didn't mean to get so worked up. I can handle things better than that usually. I had too much to drink. I am sorry."

"That's okay. You had a lot on your mind."

"That's not really a good excuse," he said, frowning.

She smiled at this. "How about some coffee?"

"Great! I was just thinking about that."

He reached for a cigarette and his lighter when he saw her make a face.

"You don't like my smoking, do you?"

"No. It's terrible for your health." She hesitated. "And it smells bad."

"Okay, okay. You always tell me what you really think. I've been thinking of quitting anyway. Maybe now is a good time."

"You mean that?" She smiled.

"Sure, why not? I don't even like the smell anymore." He fished in his pockets for the cigarette pack, and then his lighter. "Here," he gave them to her. "Just throw them out."

Gina raised her eyebrows and looked at him.

"It's okay. Throw them away. I don't want them anymore."

She took them from his hand and put them into the trash, and returned to him with a smile. "Now, how about that coffee?"

"Sure."

"Would you like some toast, too?"

"That sounds wonderful." He grinned.

They sat in silence while they drank their coffee. He buttered a piece of toast and chewed thoughtfully. "You know, I do want to apologize for last night," he began.

She waited.

"I guess the drinking is kind of a thing with Japanese men. It's like a tradition, but it's not really a good way to handle stress. I mean, when you drink too much you end up with the same problems as before, only you have a bad headache too." He leaned toward her so their foreheads touched. "I did not mean to upset you," he whispered. "Please do not think bad thoughts about me."

"I don't. Everyone needs to get their feelings out sometime. We call it venting. You know, just letting it all out. Kind of like releasing a pressure valve."

He looked relieved.

"I have to work late tonight," she said. "I'm not sure what time I'll be home. Maybe you can get some more sleep and get rid of your headache."

He smiled ruefully. "Maybe so."

* * *

When she returned home after work, Taro greeted her at the door with, "I have a surprise for you."

"Yeah?"

"How about a late night picnic?'

She was speechless.

He led her to the patio, where a table was set with candles, two sets of plates and wine glasses. More candles lined the little adobe wall behind the table, flickering against a midnight blue sky. Twinkling stars stretched to the horizon.

"How lovely!"

"I hoped you would like it. I'm not a very good cook, but I have frozen lasagna and garlic bread in the oven…"

"Where did you…"

"I walked down to the grocery store and brought some things back. There's wine in the refrigerator, too." He brought out a bottle and poured some into both glasses.

"Here's to a better night than last night," he said, touching his glass to hers. "And I have not smoked at all today. It's funny, I didn't even miss it."

She smiled at this.

"So, am I forgiven for last night?"

"Of course you are. I tried to tell you this morning."

"Good," and he winked at her. "Now let's eat!"

She laughed, and in that moment all her cares drifted away. She gazed up into a night sky cluttered with stars so close she could imagine touching one. Her spirit soared. *What a wonderful way to end the day!*

After dinner, they brought the dishes back into the house and extinguished the candles.

"And, now" Taro whispered, taking her hand, "we should go upstairs. We need to make up for last night."

All through the night, she stayed wrapped in Taro's arms, her back against his chest, her head in the hollow of his neck. She felt the gentle motion of his chest against her back as he breathed. She sighed and snuggled closer against him. *Can this be real? Is it possible to be this happy?*

She thought briefly of her other lovers and could see how one-sided all her past relationships had been. Either she had not been fully involved from a lack of commitment on her part, or she had adored her partner so excessively that part of her was always nervous, too eager to please, so she could never truly relax. Sometimes, if the relationship became too serious, she withdrew in panic, afraid the man would eventually try to change her and remake her into what he wanted, never really appreciating the qualities she had. In all of these relationships, she had never felt she could be seen for who she really was.

This time was different. Even though their origins were oceans apart, their cultures totally different, they saw each other clearly and appreciated what they saw.

Chapter 16

IN THE MORNING Gina went outside to put out food and water for the birds. She did not see Taro come to the patio. He stood watching her for a little while before saying anything. "My mother does this too, in the garden behind our house. She and my father loved that little garden, and now she walks in it alone. She says she feels close to him there."

She raised her eyebrows in surprise, and he continued, "I lost my father two years ago."

"Oh... I didn't know. I'm so sorry," she said, turning to face him. "What happened?"

My father was a salaryman. He worked too hard; and he had a heart attack.

"That happens a lot in Japan, doesn't it?"

"Yes. We call it *karoshi*, death from overwork. He wanted me to work for the same company, too, but he finally understood what music means to me. Before he died, we talked about it. He said he was proud of my success."

After a pause, he continued, "After his death, my mother told me I should do what I loved. She said I should not live life for 'someday'. My father never lived to truly enjoy his life. He worked so hard to provide for my sisters and me, but it cost him everything, and then we could never get him back."

"I am so sorry", she said again, and she touched his cheek. "But I understand." Tears stung her eyes. "I lost my father, too", she whispered.

He threw her a quick look of surprise, and she continued, "About three years ago. He was a good man, so kind and so wise. I miss him every day."

Their eyes locked in a moment of quiet sharing, pain remembered, both understanding that this sorrow was one more connection they shared.

Chapter 17

"Taro, what would you say to having dinner tonight with one of my friends from the store? She said she wants to talk with me. Something important."

"Sure, why not?"

"Oh, good. I hoped you wouldn't mind. Something's going on at the store, and I need to find out what it is. Gloria is the most popular manager there, but there have been a lot of closed-door meetings going on since last week. I have a bad feeling about it, and Gloria said she couldn't talk to me at the store."

"Okay. Do you want to meet here, or in a restaurant?'

"Let's go out. There's a nice Italian place close by. Let me call her to make sure."

When Gina and Taro arrived at the restaurant, Gloria was already there, sitting with a man Gina had never seen before. He rose to greet them. Gloria stood up and gave Gina a hug. "Oh, Gina, I'm glad you're here. This is Steve, my husband. And Steve, this is Gina, and ...?"

"Taro," Taro said, shaking hands with both of them.

Steve remarked to Taro, "You look familiar. Have I seen you before?"

"Maybe. I'm a musician and we've played here a couple of times."

"No kidding?" Steve said. "What's the name of your band?"

"Moonstorm. We've been on the road a lot this year. Right now we're touring with Hammersmith, and we have a show up in San Francisco next weekend."

"That's great!" Steve said. "I love those guys. So, tell me, is Lars Hammersmith as wild as what we hear in the media?"

"Sometimes," Taro laughed.

"Hey, Gloria, I like this guy!" Steve said, slapping Taro on the back and grinning. "This is great."

"Steve's a high school math teacher, but he loves rock and roll," Gloria explained, rolling her eyes. "He didn't really want to go out tonight, but you just made his day." She smiled at them. "Why don't we sit down?"

After they were all seated and food was ordered, Gloria glanced over her shoulder at the almost empty restaurant before she started to speak.

"Gina, the reason I wanted to see you tonight is to let you know that today was my last day at La Mode. I wanted to tell you before you got there tomorrow and found out I was gone."

Gina leaned forward in shock. "What? You quit? When did this happen?"

"About two weeks ago. I wanted to tell you about it. And warn you."

"Warn me? About what? What's going on, Gloria?"

"The Weasel is what's going on. As long as he's running the store, none of you is safe."

Taro looked confused. "What is the Weasel?"

"The store manager," Gloria and Gina said together.

"I don't understand," Taro said. "Isn't a weasel a kind of animal?"

"Yes it is," Gina said. "But it's also a name for a sneaky, bad-news lowlife who will back-stab anybody."

"Especially someone he wants to get rid of." Gloria added.

"He wanted to get rid of you?" Gina exclaimed. "I can't believe it. You're one of the best managers in the store."

"That doesn't mean anything if you get on his wrong side."

"And you did that? How?"

"I think he's been wanting to push me out for a while. Rumor has it that he has a friend in the buying office who wants that position. I'm not completely sure about that; but there were other things."

"Like what?"

"Gina, you know how he whines about everything and can really make your life miserable if you don't agree with him. He's been coming to me lately with constant complaints about one thing or another, and usually I stand up to him. I think that made him mad.

He also hates my assistant manager, Jeff, and has been pretty aggressive about trying to get him fired. He claims that there have been a lot of customer complaints about him. I asked for proof—you know, letters, or people I could call to see if there really was a problem. He has never given me one shred of evidence. I think he made it all up, and he knows I think that. It didn't exactly endear me to him. But the real clincher happened a few weeks ago when he tried to discredit me in front of the regional manager.

Steve had been sitting quietly, but turned to Gina and Taro with a furious expression. "That bastard set her up to make her look like a complete idiot in front of the big brass. What he did ruined her chances of ever being promoted again. It makes me so mad I'd like to kill him!"

"What happened?" Gina breathed.

"Gina, do you remember a few weeks back, when we had a store visit from the regional manager and old Daddy DuVall?"

"Of course I remember. Everybody in the place was stressed to the max trying to get ready for that visit."

"Wait a minute," Taro interjected. "I don't understand. What's the big deal about a visit?"

Gloria explained. "Old Daddy Philippe DuVall is the head of the DuVall family, who owns the stores. He started the business way back right after the war, when he came over from France. He inspects all the stores at least twice a year, and checks everything. Sometimes he even talks with customers. He's actually a nice old man, but when he comes, he brings a group of top executives with him, including the regional manager, and they tour the stores. Everything has to be perfect when he comes. So, you can imagine, it always causes a lot of pressure when one of his visits is coming up."

"I understand," Taro said. "But what happened this time?"

"Well, the Weasel came to me two days before the visit, and he told me I had to do a major floor move in my department. He wanted a whole new look. One of the things he wanted to do was to take down the sock wall and put all the socks in bins on a table in front of the register, so they were all up in the front of the department."

"What's a sock wall?" Taro questioned.

Gina explained. "It means a whole wall with nothing but socks and that kind of thing, small accessories, all on little pegs, completely covering a wall."

Taro looked confused, so Gloria elaborated. "You're a guy. Say you wanted to buy some new socks. If you went into a store to buy some, do you think they would be out in front, or would you usually find them in the back?"

Taro thought out loud, "I guess they would be in the back, because all the shirts and stuff would be in front. Besides, if I was just looking for socks, I would want to run in and get them and get out pretty fast."

"Exactly," Gloria agreed. "That's how most men shop. If they want something basic, like socks, they don't want to spend a lot of time looking for them. They want to get in and out. And, socks are pretty cheap—not a high dollar sale, so it makes sense to put them in a place where they don't take up valuable floor space, and all the colors and styles can be out and easy to find."

"Okay, I get it," Taro said. "That makes sense."

"Well, the Weasel told me to take down the sock wall and hang jeans up instead. Do you have any idea how many little pegs of socks I had to take down? Just think about it—all the colors, styles, and fabrics have to be together, but separated. That might not sound like much, but you have black socks, brown socks, navy socks, you know. All the colors. Then there are different sizes. Then you have dress socks, sports socks, cotton socks, nylon socks, specialty socks; you name it. There were over two, maybe three hundred little pegs. Everything had to come down, and all the socks had to be put on tables in bins. Everything had to be labeled, too. It was a nightmare. And, of course, the bins had to be checked all the time because people would mess things up and you couldn't find what you were looking for. By the time we got finished, the whole department looked like a discount store—messy and confusing. And the jeans we put on the back wall couldn't be seen well, because that area is kind of dark. We worked all day to get that done. I even had to come in on my day off, and I was there from before the store opened until we closed that night."

Gloria stopped for a moment and sipped her drink. "It was a nightmare." She shuddered.

"Oh, Gloria, I didn't know," Gina consoled. "I heard something about some big changes going on, but I never had any idea it was like that. I'm so sorry."

Gloria's eyes started to tear up, but she brushed her hand over her eyes.

"Somehow I managed to do it all, just like the Weasel wanted. By the morning of the visit, everything was done, and we were ready."

Gina and Taro exchanged a look, then leaned forward to hear the rest of the story.

"Okay, so here comes Old Daddy DuVall and the Weasel, and the regional manager, and the whole group. They came right into my department. I was there to greet them, of course."

She paused to take some more sips from her drink. "The regional manager looked confused and irritated. He walked around the tables a couple of times, then old Daddy DuVall walked around with him, and they were whispering to each other.

Then they asked me why the socks were all on tables instead of up on a wall. They said the new jeans and shirts should have been up front instead, where customers could see them easily.

And, then, in front of all those people, the Weasel said, "Gloria, I told you not to do this because it was a bad idea." David Rosenberg, the regional manager, was frowning and I could hear some comments he made to Daddy DuVall about me not being a good merchandiser.

And, of course, the Weasel told me, in front of everybody, to put a sock wall up and make some other changes. Everything would be pretty much the way it was before. I could see David Rosenberg's face. He's basically a good guy, but he never forgets anything when it goes wrong. So, right there, I knew my career with La Mode was over."

"She came home crying that night," Steve fumed. "After she stayed until closing again to put everything back. She finally had to leave because they were locking up for the night. Then, she had to be back there before the store opened the next day to finish it all. She was there until closing again that night."

"That's awful!" Taro exclaimed. "No wonder you quit."

"That bastard broke her heart," Steve declared. "After almost ten years working there. It makes me so mad I could just kill him."

"I don't blame you."

"So, what did you do about it, Gloria?" Gina patted Gloria's hand.

"Nothing. There wasn't anything I could do. It would have been his word against mine. He's the store manager, so you know who they would believe. Besides, if I had caused any trouble, I would have gotten a bad reference and could never have gotten another job. So I started looking and was lucky enough to find something else. I start on Monday."

"Are you going with another store?"

"Hell, no. Not after that. It's a good thing I've been interested in computers and artwork all this time. I got a job with an advertising agency and I'll be designing websites and promotional campaigns for a whole lot of different clients."

"But you were such a good manager," Gina pointed out. "Everybody liked you, Gloria. And you have all those years of experience in merchandising…"

"Don't worry, I'll be using all that experience in my new job," Gloria vowed. "I'm actually looking forward to making a new start. I am worried about my assistant manager, though. Once I'm gone, the Weasel will find a way to get rid of him, too. Jeff's a nice guy and is really good at what he does. Plus he has two children to support. I know the Weasel will fire him on some kind of trumped-up charge, and ruin his career, too. And there's not a thing I can do to prevent it."

"Who is this guy?" Taro exclaimed. "I can't believe that such a terrible person can be in charge. He sounds like an idiot."

"He is," the other three said together. "He's done things like this before, and killed a lot of people's careers. And they couldn't do anything about it because they needed a good reference to get another job."

"This is unbelievable. I can't think of any Japanese company that would treat its workers like this."

"Yeah, but don't a lot of people over there die from overwork?" Steve asked.

"Yes, that's true, but it's not the same. Those workers feel complete loyalty to their companies, and the companies think of their workers like a family. It would be unheard of for a manager to ridicule an employee in public like that. They would never cause a worker to lose face that way. If there are problems, it is handled in private so no one is embarrassed. That way the organization stays strong. But this Weasel guy sounds like he should be locked up. How does he get away with all of this?"

"Because people are afraid to say anything. And he keeps files on everybody so he has things he can use later if he wants to get rid of somebody," Gloria stated.

"She's right," Gina agreed. "I remember his first sales meeting, when he told us to do the same thing. He actually said that we should start documenting everyone as soon as they were hired, just in case there would be a need to fire them later."

"What?" Taro was astounded. "I've never heard of anyone doing that before. They should get rid of him. How can any company survive if the management completely demoralizes the employees? I think I'd like to punch his lights out."

"You and me both," Steve agreed.

"It's even worse than that," Gloria added. "If someone breaks a store rule, he makes sure to write it up, so he has something he can use against them. But, if he can't get evidence fast enough, he just makes stuff up, like saying there are customer complaints. If there are enough complaints, he can have someone fired, just like that." She snapped her fingers for emphasis.

"Isn't that against the law?"

"Of course. But, how could you prove it?"

Taro frowned. "Have you ever thought about doing your own documentation?" he suggested.

"What do you mean?" Gloria said, and they all turned to look at him.

"Maybe you could catch him at his own game. If he comes to you with some crazy idea, try to get it in writing from him. Then you have something you can use against him. If he wants you do something you think is a bad idea, maybe you could say you don't understand and ask him to email you or something. Then you'd have his instructions and a date on it."

Gloria smiled. "That's a good idea."

"There has to be some way you can protect yourself from a person like that," Taro continued. If he has been doing this kind of thing a long time, he has probably grown careless. That would make it easier to catch him in his own trap."

Gloria and Steve looked at each other and grinned. "I tell you, I like this guy!" Steve exclaimed.

Steve ordered another round of drinks, and they finished their dinners in better spirits.

The two men wandered over to the dessert bar to look at the possibilities there, giving Gloria and Gina a few moments alone.

"Wow, Gina, where did you find him?" Gloria expressed in admiration.

"It's a long story."

"I'm sure. You've been holding out on us. I like him. He's nice. Smart, too. And, he is incredibly good-looking."

"I had noticed that," Gina teased.

"Hmmmmm," Gloria mused. "He's really kind of exotic looking. Beautiful eyes. I like the long hair too; it looks good on him."

Gloria glanced over at Taro, who was talking with Steve, and then back to Gina. "The two of you look good together," she decided. "You've got that short white-blonde hair going on and those huge eyes, and his hair is so dark, but you're both tall and slim and you seem really comfortable together. Somehow your differences enhance each other."

"Thanks, Gloria," Gina whispered. "We're good together. I'm not sure how it happened exactly, but I think we're happy."

"Looks like it," Gloria said.

Taro returned to the table. "I got you some ice cream. Vanilla," he said to Gina. He settled into his chair. "I thought maybe we can talk about something good for a while, like ice cream and new friends." He smiled.

Gina could tell that Gloria was charmed.

Before the evening was over, Gloria added, "One more thing, Gina. Please be careful. You have two sets of buyers to keep happy, and those ladies do not like each other. Don't get caught in the crossfire."

"What is she talking about?" Taro asked.

"I got promoted to run two different departments, and they're on different floors. There are two different groups of buyers, and naturally, they each want all my attention and effort to promote their merchandise, not anyone else's. So they keep me running up and down the stairs all day trying to keep up with their demands. And of course, I get no support at all from the Weasel. If I'm working downstairs with the accessories department, he will show up and whine that I'm neglecting the other department, and so I have to run up there and see what's going on. It's hard to finish any project without interruptions, so a lot of the time I come in early or on my days off to catch up."

Taro frowned. "I don't like the sound of that."

"Nobody would," Gloria snapped. "It's an impossible situation, but they're too cheap to hire another manager like they should. "She's the only manager in the store who has to handle two different areas."

She warned again, "Just be careful. Don't give the Weasel anything to complain about. And, if I were you, I would start thinking about what else you can do, so you'll have a backup plan in case."

"Actually, I do," Gina confided. "I've been selling jewelry in some of the boutiques over in Scottsdale."

"I heard about that," Gloria admitted. "Lynn told me. She was excited about it. But, if the Weasel ever found out, he could claim you have a conflict of interest. So be careful. By the way, you can trust Lynn.

She's a real friend, and you might not know this, but her aunt is married to old Daddy Duvall's oldest son. She's one of the few managers the Weasel won't dare touch." Gloria thought for a moment, and added, "One other person he won't dare to mess with is Carmen, the cosmetics manager."

"Why?" Taro questioned.

"Because Carmen is Mexican, and her husband is a hotshot civil rights attorney. The Weasel doesn't want a discrimination suit on his hands."

"This store sounds like a battlefield," Taro commented. "Terrible. Are all American stores like this?"

"No, I don't think so. Or, hopefully, not as bad as this."

The four of them talked another hour or so, and the mood gradually brightened. There were a lot of jokes about ice cream, especially because Taro went back for more. "He has a fondness for ice cream," Gina explained. "Especially chocolate."

At the end of the evening, there were hugs and handshakes all around, and plans made to keep in touch.

Gina was yawning already, so Taro drove them back to her house.

"You have to go into work early tomorrow, don't you?" he asked her.

"Yes, but I wish I could just stay home. With you."

Taro grinned. "Don't worry. I'll be here when you get home. But tonight, I think you should just sleep."

"Okay," she yawned. "Sleep."

* * *

Just before dawn, Gina woke up. Taro was sitting up, staring at her.

"What's the matter? Couldn't sleep?" she whispered.

"No, not much." He pulled her closer so her head rested on his chest.

"Why not?"

"I was thinking about everything I heard at dinner and I'm worried about you. Your store is a strange place. Until last night I had no idea of the kind of pressure you must face every day. I don't want you to ever be treated like your friend Gloria. And I really do not like that Weasel person."

She rose up on an elbow to look at him. "That's really sweet."

She lowered her head back onto his chest and felt his arms wrap around her. "Taro, don't worry. Just try to sleep, okay?" she whispered.

"All right."

Chapter 18

GINA STORMED IN and slammed the door. "*Baka kuso atama!*" she muttered under her breath.

Taro mouthed the words silently, staring at her and trying not to laugh.

"Stupid. Shit. Head?" He raised his eyebrows. "Where did you come up with that?"

"I just put it together," she said, as her cheeks turned red. "I've been listening to you, and looking words up." She held out an English-Japanese dictionary. "I wanted to learn some Japanese and surprise you."

He laughed, shaking his head.

"Is it correct?"

"Well, I guess so. Is that really what you want to say? It's not very polite."

"It's not meant to be. I'm talking about the Weasel."

A sly smile crept across his face. "I'll have to keep an eye on you. You're dangerous with a dictionary." He reached for her, pulling her close. "What else have you learned?"

"I guess you'll just have to wait around and find out," she teased.

"Actually, that reminds me about something I want to talk about," he said.

"Okay, what?"

"Something serious. I've been thinking about the situation in your store, and I'm worried about this Weasel. I don't think he is a good person and he can't be trusted. You need to be protected."

"Protected how?"

"By being mindful of what you are dealing with, and knowing some strategies to protect yourself against him."

"Okay, you've got my attention. What do you have in mind? By the way, I'm hungry. I was thinking about fixing some fried chicken for dinner."

"No, not tonight." He frowned. "Let's just have something simple. I want you to listen to some ideas about how you can protect yourself. I don't think the store is a good place for you to be."

"Oh. Well, there's some ground beef in the refrigerator. How about some burgers?"

Taro's face lit up. "That's fine with me. "I just want us to have some time to talk tonight." He watched as she chopped onions and made hamburger patties. She set the oven to broil and mixed a salad while they waited for the oven to heat up.

"Why do you put them in the oven? I thought you cook them on top of the stove."

Gina smiled. "I think they taste better this way, and they aren't so greasy.

"Oh, okay."

While they waited for the broiler, Gina scooped the salad into bowls and Taro took them out to the table. He returned to the kitchen and stood watching her.

When the burgers were done, they went out to the table to eat.

"Really good," Taro said, after taking several bites. "Better than going out." He winked at her.

She grinned back at him. "Yeah, not bad. So, what did you want to talk to me about?"

He got to his point quickly. "Gina, I am worried about you and do not trust that weasel person. You need documentation, but you need to know some strategies, too."

Gina nodded, encouraging him to continue.

"When I was a schoolboy in Tokyo, I studied Kendo, with all the other boys in my class."

She looked up in surprise. "Really? I've heard of that. It's a pretty intense form of martial arts, isn't it?"

"Yeah. It can be deadly."

Taro paused to finish his burger. "There's a reason why students wear protective masks that cover their whole faces." He sighed. "I wasn't really interested in learning about fighting, but I learned a few defensive techniques." He stopped for a moment, took her hands in his and leaned toward her.

"The point is, when you study the martial arts the first thing you learn is how to avoid combat. You only fight to defend yourself. But you must always be on alert.

"We studied a two-thousand year old book written by a famous Chinese general named Sun Tsu called 'The Art of War'. He said that battle must be avoided if at all possible, but sometimes, there is no other option. He taught that you must never let the enemy know what you are thinking. Instead, study the weakness of the enemy so you will know where to strike. He said that an enemy who grows complacent lets his guard down, because of his own arrogance. That is a fatal mistake."

"Okay, that makes sense," Gina agreed. "This two thousand year old general was pretty smart."

"Yeah," Taro grinned. "That's why people study his writings today. Another thing he wrote is very interesting. He said that in battle, always leave an option open for the enemy. If you push a desperate enemy too hard, he may do something unpredictable, and that could cause you to lose the battle. So, always leave an opportunity for the enemy to save face. Try to go along with him as much as possible so you avoid a confrontation. But if he presses you into a situation where you are forced to defend yourself, keep calm and be decisive."

"Let's Google this guy. What's his name? Sun Tsu?"

"Yeah. His ideas about war are used in business now. I don't know this Weasel person, so I don't know why he acts the way he does. But he sacrifices his own people, so I think he must be unsure of his own position. He must be desperate to look good to those above him, and that makes him dangerous. From what your friend told you, he has learned how to get rid of people so he can replace them with others who are loyal to him. This alone shows weakness. A strong leader can work with others who do not always agree with him. He can listen to opposing ideas with no threat to his own position. Your Weasel is not strong, and so he can turn against anyone at any time. This makes him a threat to you and any future you have with that company."

"So what do you think I should do?"

"Do not show your feelings about him. Try to agree with him whenever you can, but keep a record. Unfortunately for your friend, she did not, so she was not prepared when he made his move against her. You, however, know he cannot be trusted. You can be prepared."

"I hate all this kind of stuff," she complained. "It makes everything at work so much more difficult."

"I know. I don't like it either, but I want to know you can take care of yourself. I would be upset if anyone ever hurt you, but I'm not always here with you, and I worry."

After dinner, Taro volunteered to wash the dishes while Gina went to the computer. She called Taro to see what she found on the internet. "He's here! Your Chinese general. Look at all this information about him." She pointed to the screen.

Taro pulled up a chair next to her.

"Look at these quotes from him." Gina was excited. "It's just like what you told me. This is excellent advice."

Taro hugged her. "Remember this. I want you to be safe."

She turned to him with a kiss. "Thank you for being so concerned for me."

His eyes glittered. "So, now we have this two-thousand year old secret. Don't forget."

"Speaking of secrets," she teased, changing the subject. "I have some ice cream hidden in the freezer for you. Chocolate."

"It's my favorite," he laughed. "Can we have some now?"

"Sure."

Chapter 19

TARO MET HER AT THE DOOR as she came in. "You're really late tonight. Is everything all right?"

She hugged him tightly before she spoke. "Taro, I did something today that could get me fired."

"Tell me," he urged. "What happened?" He pulled out a chair and motioned for her to sit at the table.

"I broke a major company rule today." She looked over at him. He waited, his eyes huge with concern.

Gina took a deep breath. "I caught a girl shoplifting, and I didn't turn her over to store security."

Taro raised his eyebrows but said nothing.

"I saw her try to hide behind a rack and stuff some clothes into a bag. She wasn't a very good thief. It was pretty obvious she had never done anything like that before. So I walked up to her and told her I saw what she did, and I took her into my office."

Gina shook her head. "I don't know why I did that. There was just something about her, the sad, scared look she had. Something. Anyhow, I got everything back, and instead of calling security, I talked to her. I wanted to know why she did it."

"What did she say?"

"It turned out the girl wasn't a bad kid, just very unhappy. She's a pretty good student, but she's been bullied at school by some of the popular kids. She told me she hasn't had anyone to turn to since her mother died a few years ago. Her father is still consumed with grief over the death of the mother. He spends all his energy on work and shuts out his daughter. Her older sister is married and busy with kids of her own, so this girl has been alone for a long time. She told me she thought if she had some stylish clothes to wear, maybe the other kids would be nicer to her. All she wanted was just to fit in. She was just fourteen years old. It was so sad."

"So what did you do?"

"I called her father and he came into the store to meet with me. That's why I was so late getting home tonight. He's some kind of executive in a big company, and had absolutely no idea that his daughter was so unhappy. When he found out what happened, he broke down and cried, and thanked me for doing what I did. We had a long talk. I explained how serious this situation could have been, and how it could have messed up his daughter for life. The girl promised to never steal again, and the father promised to spend more time with his daughter. He even bought the clothes she had tried to steal."

Gina gulped. "So, what do you think? Did I do the right thing?"

Taro grabbed her in a hug. "Yes, Gina. Absolutely. The poor kid had problems already, so how could turning her in have helped anything?"

"And you don't even know how some of those store security guys can be," Gina continued. "Some of them are real jerks. Like wanna-be cops, only not smart enough to get into real police work. Everything for them is either black or white—no mercy. That kid would have wound up in juvenile detention with a police record for the rest of her life. She seemed to be kind of sensitive, and basically a good kid; I don't think she would have ever recovered."

Taro reached for Gina's hands. He leaned toward her. "I think you have the kindest heart of anyone I have ever known."

"Really?" Gina whispered. She brushed back tears. "I just couldn't do it. Something about that girl made me think she deserved better."

"I agree," Taro said. "Does anyone else know about this? You don't want that Weasel person to find out."

"Yeah, no kidding. He'd fire me for sure."

"Well, I'll never tell him." He winked.

"Let's go out somewhere for dinner," he suggested. "How about a Japanese place? I've been thinking about sushi."

"Sounds great. I've heard about a place called Zen Garden, but I've never been there."

"Well, then, let's go."

* * *

The restaurant was located in an upscale shopping center with stunning views of the surrounding mountains. As they crossed the parking lot, Gina noticed a new shop.

"Let's go in here. I've heard a lot about this place."

"Treasures and Trinkets?" Taro read on the sign. "What kind of store is this?"

"Competition. It's a new jewelry chain that just opened here. I want to take a look at what they have."

They walked in and strolled down the aisles.

"Well, no big problem," Gina whispered. "Most of this stuff is just cheap costume jewelry. It looks like it's designed mostly for teenagers."

She stopped in front of a display case featuring a sign that read "Genuine Imitations."

"Wow!" she exclaimed in surprise. "Look at these! Fake diamond earrings and engagement rings."

Taro scrutinized the display. "These look real," he agreed.

"Yeah, they do. It would be hard to tell the difference without a really close look. I love that emerald cut —really classy looking. And the earrings are pretty. We have some like this, but they're rhinestones. I'll have to talk with the buying office about this place."

She straightened up. "Okay. I've seen enough. Are you ready to eat now? I'm getting hungry."

"Me, too." Taro smiled. "It has been a long time since I had sushi. Let's go." He took her arm and they walked across the parking lot to the restaurant.

She liked the place immediately, appreciating the subdued dark atmosphere. Colorful paper lanterns illuminated the tables. She noticed

Taro scanning the interior, a huge grin across his face. "Look, they have a patio, too. And it's empty. Let's have dinner out there."

They were seated, and Taro leaned across the little table. "I think we should start by ordering some Japanese beer. You may not know this, but Japan has been making beer for centuries. Much longer than most of the rest of the world. It's good, too."

"Two bottles of Kirin, please," he said to the waiter.

"Is that your favorite?"

"One of them. I like Sapporo, too. Let's relax for a while before we eat. I want to talk with you about what happened today."

He pulled his chair closer. "I've been thinking about that kid you helped. I like how you handled it."

"Thanks."

He leaned closer and touched his forehead to hers. "I think something about her must have touched a memory in you, *ne?*"

"You may be right." She hesitated, gathering her thoughts. *As usual, he seems to know what I'm thinking, and he understands.*

He waited.

Gina sighed. "I had a hard time fitting in as a kid. We moved so much, I was always the new kid, trying to be accepted. It wasn't easy. Sometimes I was very lonely. My family was always too busy to pay much attention to me. I bet that's really different from your experience, huh?"

"*So, yo.* Japan is a small country, compared to here. My family has lived in the same area for generations, and I had friends that I grew up with."

He paused for a moment and ordered two more beers from the waiter before he continued. "But friends can grow apart. That hurts, I know. Sometimes I was lonely, too." He suddenly stopped talking. Gina noticed his brows had pushed together into a frown. His face had assumed a vacant expression, as if he had been transported far away, or back to another time.

Where have his thoughts taken him?

He pulled himself back to the present and focused on her. "But my experience is nothing like yours. When your family moved, it was thousands of miles away. America is such a big country. Now that I've seen a lot of it, I understand how hard that must have been for you. I'm sure you always tried to make new friends everywhere you went. And you were willing to take a chance with me, even though I'm from another country."

Gina met his eyes. "Otherwise I would never have met you."

"I know," Taro said. He leaned closer and gave her a quick kiss.

He straightened up when the waiter appeared with more beer and a sample plate of sushi.

Gina hesitated, looking at the choices. Which one would be best to start with?

Taro's eyes twinkled as he watched her. "Here, try some of this. I think you will like it." He leaned to her with a sushi roll in his fingers.

She opened her mouth to taste the sushi, and her teeth came down gently on his fingers. Instantly realizing what she had done, she licked where she had just bitten his skin, and rolled her eyes up to meet his.

"M-mmmm you taste good. So does the sushi."

His eyes were intense as he gazed at her and smiled.

Several hours later, Gina caught herself fighting back a yawn, but Taro noticed it. He grinned. "We should go. It's getting late and you must be tired."

She nodded and smiled. "Yeah, I am, but I feel so relaxed now. This night was exactly what I needed."

"I'm glad."

They stood up and Taro leaned over to whisper in her ear, "But now, I want to be back in your house, in your bed, and in you."

Gina blushed and peeked around to be sure nobody had overheard.

"One of these days I need to talk to you about your shyness," she teased. She pretended to look down in modesty, but then batted her eyelashes as she looked back up at him.

Taro met her eyes and grinned.

He paid the bill and they left the restaurant. Outside, the parking lot was almost deserted. Above them, the sky was filled with stars and Gina could not resist turning to him. "Dance with me," she whispered.

Taro took her hand and turned her in circles toward him, and they moved together across the pavement.

Gina gazed up. "Look at all those stars. It's kind of like the first time you danced with me."

"Yeah, it is," Taro agreed. "That was the first time I held you. Under a sky full of stars." He began to hum a melody and turned her toward him again. When they reached Gina's Jeep, he opened the door for her. Before she got in, he wrapped his hands around her face and kissed her.

"Wow, that was some kiss," Gina managed to say before he kissed her again.

"Let's go home." His voice was husky.

Taro parked the Jeep in front of her house and helped her out. Once they were inside, he pushed the door closed and leaned into her with a kiss.

She sensed an urgency in him that thrilled her to her core. "Let's go upstairs," she breathed. As they rushed up the stairs, Gina did not notice the steps under her feet. It was more like flying.

When they reached the bedroom, Taro pulled her into his arms, spreading kisses across her face.

"Taro," she breathed, kissing him, too, inhaling the scent of him.

Taro backed her toward the bed, reaching down the front of her blouse, undoing every button as he went. He pulled the blouse free from her body and tossed it aside, and they tumbled together onto the bed. He reached for the zipper on her jeans and pulled it down as far as it would go and tugged at the fabric until it began to slide down her hips. She arched her back, bringing her legs up enough that Taro could pull her jeans all the way down and off the ends of her feet.

She sat up to gaze at him, wearing only her bra and panties, and watched him undress. "I like looking at you," she whispered.

"It's too dark in here," he muttered. He rose and walked across to the dresser, lit a candle, and turned back to her before placing the candle on the dresser.

The sight of Taro, stark naked, illuminated by the candleglow, was enough to catch Gina's breath in her throat. He stood before her, completely naked, gloriously male, fully erect, a sculpture crafted by a master craftsman, a study in black and white.

No, nothing crafted by mankind could ever create such exquisite beauty. Only God could create something so perfect.

She drank in the sight of him, his perfect body with his strong shoulders and arms, slim legs, flat belly, creamy-looking skin, beautiful dark eyes, glossy black hair, and perfect white teeth. His eyes softened as he looked at her.

"My sweet Gina," he whispered, moving to close the distance between them. He reached for her hands, pulling her to her feet and then leaning down to unhook her bra and pull down her panties.

"Gina, I want so much to be inside you right now." He kissed down her neck to her breasts, licking and sucking until she moaned, then lifted her onto the bed and positioned himself at her side, kissing her all down the length of her body.

Oh my God, I want this man.

She could feel herself growing moist as a sensation of emptiness overwhelmed her, painfully, crying to be filled.

"Taro, I want you, too. So much."

He moved to cover her with his body, reaching down to position himself inside her and they began their dance of love.

* * *

Late in the night, Gina jolted awake. For a few seconds, she was confused, not sure exactly where she was. She flashed through memories of every place she had ever lived. She ran her hand through her hair as she focused, and realized she was in her own bed, her own house.

She had pulled away from Taro. Outside the warmth of his arms, she shivered.

He lay at her side, awake. "Bad dream?"

She nodded, feeling cold and embarrassed. "For a few minutes I wasn't sure where I was," she confided. "I guess all that talking about moving around as a child really stirred up memories."

"Has this happened before?"

"Sometimes," she admitted, pulling away in embarrassment.

Taro lifted her chin and gazed directly into her eyes.

"It's all right," he soothed, bringing her closer until her head rested on his chest. "It's all right. You are here, and I am here. We are together, and you are safe."

She moved closer into the warmth of his body and felt him wrap his arms around her.

Relief spread through her senses.

He rolled over with her still in his arms.

"Gina, go back to sleep now," he whispered. "You are safe and everything is all right. And if you have any more bad dreams, I will be here to chase them away."

End of Book 1

The story continues

Moon Music 2 Coming Soon.

"WHERE ARE YOU?"

"In the men's room at LAX Airport. No one knows I have a cell phone with me." Taro sighed. "Our visas expired and we're waiting for a flight to Tokyo. Someone is with us to make sure we get on the plane."

"You mean, like a guard?"

"Yes."

"Oh, no!" Gina groaned. "If you get on that plane, you might never come back." *This is awful. What I most dreaded to hear. There has to be some way around this.*

"Let me think – you said LAX, right?"

"Yeah."

There was a long moment of silence while she tried to think of a solution.

"Okay," she announced. "LAX. That place is always a freak show. So many crazy looking people pass through there every day no one pays any attention. You've got to get out of there. Do not get on that plane."

"How?"

"Find some way to start a diversion and slip away."

"What?"

"Just find a way to get out – right now. Run if you have to. Escape and come back here," she implored. "We'll figure something out."

About the author

AURORA DAWNING has been reading and writing stories since she was a child. She has always been interested in the "What if?" Possibilities that occur in a lifetime, and the idea that sometimes, one event can change a person's destiny forever. She has traveled extensively and found that the basic need people have to be loved and understood is a universal element in all of us.

In addition to writing, she is interested in animal welfare causes.

She currently resides in the Pacific Northwest.

CPSIA information can be obtained
at www.ICGtesting.com
Printed in the USA
FSOW02n0936101016
25962FS